DRIVE ME WILD

RIGGS BROTHERS, BOOK 1

JULIE KRISS

ISBN: 978-0-9959675-9-5

Cover by Mayhem Cover Creations

Photo by Sara Eirew Photographer

❀ Created with Vellum

PROLOGUE

Emily

Eight Years Ago

NO MATTER how many times I did this, the excitement was always the same. The thrill of parking a block away, sneaking down the street, and knocking on Luke Riggs' door in the dark.

Maybe because it was forbidden. Maybe because it was fun. I hadn't stopped to analyze it, even though I'd been doing this all summer. I should probably be sorry, but I wasn't.

The door opened, and Luke was there. Westlake, Michigan's bad boy, right here on the wrong side of the tracks. Eighteen, muscled and dark, a tattoo snaking down his right arm. Irresistible, at least to me.

He lived in the guest house on his family's run-down property. A guest house sounds rich, but the Riggs were far from it. The house might have been nice once, but it wasn't anymore. Not that I cared about that. I only cared that the guest house gave us privacy.

Instead of inviting me in, Luke leaned against the door frame. He was wearing low-slung jeans and a well-worn black tee. He had the beginnings of a scowl on his face. "I didn't think you were coming," he said.

"I almost didn't," I admitted. "I still have a lot to do to get ready for tomorrow."

"Leaving for college is a big deal." His voice was flat, not his usual sexy drawl, but I barely noticed. I was impatient, distracted, my heart thumping in my chest the way it always did around Luke.

"It'll be fine," I said. "The car is mostly packed, and... Are you going to let me in?"

He watched my face for a long minute from his dark eyes. "You sure you want to come in?"

He was in a strange mood tonight. It couldn't be because I was leaving for college tomorrow, because we'd always known that would happen. We'd hooked up this past summer with high school finally over, and going to college was always in my plan. Besides, Luke and I weren't serious. No one even knew we were seeing each other. We were just having fun.

"Of course I'm sure, silly," I said. I put my hands on his flat stomach—I could feel the muscles through his T-shirt, yum—and pushed him backward. He let me, moving back out of the doorway so I could come in. I closed the door behind me.

Now we were alone. We'd done this a lot, Luke and me, over the past few months—starting with making out, then progressing to sex. He was my first, a decision I hadn't taken lightly and still didn't regret. Even now, with my virginity long gone, I felt a pulse of excitement between my legs just being near him.

This would be the last time, and then I'd go to college. I was excited about that, too. College was going to be awesome. But I couldn't leave without seeing Luke again.

I leaned up into him—he was warm and smelled wonderful—and kissed him. He kissed me back, cupping my head with one of his big hands, then broke it. "When do you leave tomorrow?" he asked, still holding onto me. There was only one lamp on in the corner of the room, and his face was shadows in the half-dark.

Why was he still on this topic? "Early," I said, putting my palms on his stomach again, this time sliding them up beneath his shirt. "We have to be quick."

"I'm never quick," he said, with a hint of his usual sexy humor. I felt part of me unwind with relief. This was the Luke I knew, and I really, really liked him.

And I wasn't going to see him again.

I was fine with it. I mean, college. I was going to college, and I was going to kick ass at it, and then I was going to get a big high-powered job. Maybe I'd buy a big house and get a high-powered husband and have a few gorgeous babies. I hadn't decided on that part. I wanted to get to college first.

"What are you going to do?" I asked Luke. "After I leave, I mean."

Luke wasn't going to college. He was a Riggs, and no Riggs ever went to college. He didn't have the grades, and he didn't have the money. His dad owned an auto body shop in town. He dropped his hands from me, tilting his head. "You've never asked me that," he said.

That mood again. "Well, I'm asking now."

"I could work in the body shop, I guess," Luke said, "but I think I might go for a drive."

I blinked at him. "Go for a drive? Where?"

"Nowhere. Anywhere. Just get in my car, hit the gas, and keep going."

I thought about that. "You mean get the hell out of Westlake."

"Pretty much."

It was a common feeling. Westlake didn't have much going for it. I should know, because my mother was a cop here. She thought Westlake was great; I just wanted to put it in my rear view mirror. "You should do it," I said. "Go see the country. You could work just about anywhere." Luke knew how to fix cars, so he could get a job in a body shop wherever he went.

He looked at me again, that strange look. "You think I should do it?"

"Of course I do," I said. "But first..." I stood back with a dramatic flourish and pulled my shirt off over my head. "A proper goodbye."

I was trying to cheer him up, but he just crossed his arms and looked me up and down, his gaze pausing on my skimpy lace bra. "Is that all you got?" he said, his voice dropped a notch.

"Come on," I said, pointing to my boobs. "You love these."

"Maybe a little," he admitted.

"A lot," I corrected him, with the authority of a woman who knows. "Now it's your turn."

I was trying to get him to take his shirt off, because—oh, my lord. It didn't matter how many times I'd seen it, it still made me stop breathing for a second. He obliged me by pulling his tee off and dropping it on the floor, and I took in his muscles, his perfect tawny skin, the dusting of hair in a line below his belly button.

You aren't going to see this anymore, a voice in the back of my mind said. *This is the last time.*

I felt a pang behind my ribcage, and for a second my throat closed. But that was stupid. This was nothing. It had always been nothing. We were just having fun.

It was hormones and boredom and the lure of the forbidden. That was all it was.

But now Luke was coming toward me, and he tossed me on

my back on the bed. "Your turn," he said, and though the words were playful, his voice wasn't. His voice said something else.

I put my fingers on the buttons of my shorts, and I looked up at him, braced over me, his dark eyes fixed on me. Not on my body, on my face. Always on my face.

My throat closed again, but I forced the words out. "One last time," I said to him.

"One last time," he agreed.

I'd have one last time with Luke Riggs, and then I'd go to college.

And everything would be fine.

ONE

Emily

Present Day

THE ROAD to hell is paved with good intentions, but the road to Westlake, Michigan is paved with shame. Those of us who tried to get out—and didn't quite make it—end up on a bumpy two-lane stretch of blacktop in the middle of nowhere, headed for the town they never wanted to see again.

Or maybe that was just me.

I adjusted my aviators under the June sun and tried to act like a woman who was cool with the fact that she was coming back home after eight years. I figured a woman who was cool with it would be relaxed in the driver's seat of her old—let's say well-used—Tercel, her hands easy on the wheel, the radio playing as her tires ate up this long, empty mile of road. Even though there was no one else in the car with me, I didn't act like a woman silently freaking out that after an expensive college education and an attempt at a career, she was a flop at twenty-six. Instead, I acted like a woman who has got this fucking *down*.

I could fake that. I was good at it. And my life wasn't really over. As Mom would say: *Emily, you're being dramatic again.* I wasn't dead or sick or starving. I was just a college graduate with a load of debt, no job, and no prospects. A girl who was supposed to make good, but instead was coming back to Westlake because her sister needed help—and her parents were offering free room and board.

Even though this was supposed to be a short-term fix, it had been depressingly easy to close up my life in Illinois after my last internship burned out. I didn't have a husband, kids, a boyfriend, or even a dog to manage. I just had to notify my roommate, pack my things, load my Tercel, and head back to Westlake to help my twin sister, Lauren. She ran a hair salon in Westlake and she claimed she desperately needed a break. Cue Emily. I was surprised at the request and a little confused, since Lauren had always had everything together. But Lauren was also tight-lipped over the phone, so I'd pry more out of her in person.

I'd left the empty farmland and this part of the road was getting thicker with trees, thick scrub, and evergreens. Westlake was on the shore of Lake Michigan, and it liked to call itself a tourist town, though the truth was there were a lot nicer tourist towns on this stretch. So even with summer starting, there wasn't any traffic on this road. Just trees and blue sky and the occasional deer—I kept to the speed limit and took it slow on the bends, just in case.

And yeah, okay, it was kind of nice. I could admit that. The air smelled good when I cracked my window. Westlake was boring, but it was summer, which meant bonfires and barbecues and windy days on the beach with sand in your hair. At least, it had in my teenage memories. But you never knew. This didn't have to be all bad. Maybe there would be—

I jumped as something made a loud *clang* inside my car. Deep inside my car. There had been a sound for the last hundred miles, a sort of whirring, but I'd done the usual: prayed and ignored it. Now the sound got louder and there was a series of skidding thuds that sounded like bad news. Beneath my hands, the wheel did a little shimmy, like it was trying to get away.

"Fuck," I said aloud to no one. "Fuck, fuck, *fuck.*" My little car was ten years old, and it wasn't aging very well. I gripped the wheel tighter and eased off the accelerator. My car kept going, but it didn't have much heart in it. In fact, it sounded like it was thinking about giving up. I had no idea what had gone wrong, but I had about half a mile before I was stranded at the side of the road.

My mind raced. Where was I, exactly? How far from town? I had my cell, but I had no idea if I was close enough to get cell service. I mentally ticked through the landmarks I'd passed, recognizing them without realizing it. The sign pointing to Four Points Cabins was a mile behind me. That meant the town limits were around five miles ahead. There wasn't much between here and there, except—

Right. Now I remembered. There was a gas station up ahead. At least, there had been eight years ago—I hoped to hell it was still there. It wasn't much more than a gas bar and a counter displaying some packs of gum and Slim Jims, but it was someplace to pull over, and—please, God—maybe get help. I tapped the accelerator, wincing at the sound my engine made when I tried to goose my car along. Fuck, this was bad. Very, very bad.

And probably expensive. But I couldn't think about that right now.

I leaned forward, as if I could coax my car along like a

limping horse. "Come on," I urged it. "Come on. I need just a little luck here. Come on..."

I almost made it. Almost.

My car coughed to a stop just as I could see the sign for the gas station up ahead. I coaxed my dead vehicle onto the gravel at the side of the road and got out. I kicked the tires and shouted *Fuck* a few more times, because there was no one around to see. I checked my phone and saw the battery was dead, so I shouted *Fuck* a few more times for good measure. Then I opened the back of the car and rifled through my luggage, picking out the things I'd need for the walk to the gas station.

Not one car passed me as I made the sweaty trek along the side of the road. Not that I would have taken a ride from a stranger, but still. It was like I had left Illinois and gone to the moon, except I was wearing jeans and ankle boots and a T-shirt with a plaid button-down thrown over it. It had been a good outfit when I'd gotten into my car in the chill of early morning. Now sweat poured down my back and I took off the plaid shirt, tying it around my waist as my boots kicked the gravel. I twisted my blonde hair up off my neck into a sweaty ponytail, yanking my hair as strands blew in my face.

I sighed hard. This sucked, but I had to remember what was important. My mom was getting an Award of Merit from the Westlake police force—she was Westlake's only female police officer, then police sergeant, in history. There was going to be a big ceremony and everything, and I needed to be there.

And even more importantly, Lauren needed me. We weren't identical twins—we were fraternal—but we were twins nonetheless. She was the together one, the one who had married her high school boyfriend and bought a little bungalow and started a business. I was the one who stayed single, didn't even have a boyfriend to bring home, and had gone off to college to find a bigger life. It went against nature that Lauren was the one who needed help and I was the one to help her, but I would do it for her. For a little while.

A little while. Right.

I had no idea how long I would be in Westlake. Maybe a few weeks, maybe months. It was weird, not knowing what my future would be. It was sort of freeing, but it also felt a lot like giving up.

Or at least it would. If I ever got back to town at all.

"YEAH, NO," the guy behind the counter at the gas station said. "I don't think we can do that."

I stared at him. He was about my age and vaguely familiar— we'd probably gone to high school together. He had longish, tousled brown hair and the bloodshot eyes that were the sure sign he'd smoked at least one joint out back today. "You won't let me plug in my phone so I can make a call?" I asked. I'd grabbed my phone charger from the car before I'd started the long hike, half an hour ago.

He shrugged. "I'm not the boss," he said. "The only outlet is in the back, and I'm not allowed to have customers back there."

I tried not to grit my teeth. "Is there a phone here I can use, then?"

"No," he said. "We got rid of the pay phone a long time ago. Land line, too. The only phone we have here is mine."

God, this was painful. I looked him in his bloodshot eyes. "Please," I said clearly, politely. "Can I use your phone?"

But he just frowned at me, distracted. "I know you from somewhere, right?" he said. "You're from around here." His softened memory dredged it up from the depths. "You're one of the Parker sisters. The blonde one. Emily. Emily Parker."

I winced. I'd always been known as *the blonde one*, though I had to give him a little credit for remembering my name while baked eight years later. "Yeah, that's me," I said.

"I'm Ed MacGregor," the guy said. "I was a year behind you. I had a crush on both you and your sister." He smiled.

I smiled back politely, but only politely. I could tell by his expression what was coming next, and I was going to have to shut it down. Not because I was such hot shit, or because Ed MacGregor, stoned or not, was so awful. But because I'd sworn off men and dating seven months ago, and honestly, it had been the best seven months of my life.

I'd originally done it out of frustration after yet another go-nowhere short-term relationship—*No more, forget it, I'm never doing this again.* It was a fit of drama, but it only took a few weeks for me to realize how freeing it was. I no longer had to care what guys would think of what I wore, how I wore my hair, how I acted. I didn't have to go to bars anymore. I deleted the profiles I'd made on dating sites and didn't think about them again. I didn't worry about whether I was in a bad mood, or swearing too much, or puffy with PMS. And I didn't beat myself up for being single at twenty-six, because I *liked* being single. I did what I wanted, ate what I wanted, watched what I wanted. And no one had a say.

And when the odd guy showed interest and asked me out, all I had to say was *No thanks.* I didn't owe anyone an explanation. I was free.

Behind me, the digital bell beeped as the gas station door opened and another customer came in. Great, someone else got to witness this awkward moment. Maybe this person would let me borrow their phone.

"Hey Emily," Ed said, as if he was just coming up with the idea, instead of telegraphing it from a mile away. "If you're in town, we should get together sometime. Have a drink or something."

The trick, I'd learned, was to do it fast and firm. "Thanks, but no."

Behind me, the other customer opened the door of the cooler along the back wall, picking out a drink.

"It'll be fun," Ed said, as if I hadn't spoken. "We could go to the Fire Pit, like everyone did in high school. We could hang out."

The Fire Pit was a non-alcoholic diner-sandwich hangout used by every high schooler in Westlake. I'd lived half of high school there, but the idea of going there at twenty-six seemed creepy. I tried putting the words in a different order for Ed MacGregor. "No thanks. I'd really just like to call a tow truck for my car."

"It will be fun," Ed insisted as the cooler door banged shut behind me. "You look exactly the same. I mean good, of course. You look good." He smiled again.

The other customer approached the counter behind me, and for some reason the back of my neck prickled, but I didn't turn my head. "Ed," I said, giving it to him straight. "I'm not going out with you. I'm only here to make a call about my car."

Now Ed frowned. "I'm just being nice. You should be flattered."

Why did guys always say that when you turned them down? "Yeah, well, it isn't you. I've sworn off men." I didn't know why the words came out of me, and immediately I wanted to kick myself. *Don't explain, Emily. No is the only thing you have to say.*

"Wow," Ed said. "Does that mean you're into women?"

"No," came a voice beside my shoulder as the other customer leaned forward. "I don't think it does."

Every nerve in my body went on high alert. I felt myself tense. It wasn't. It couldn't be. No way.

But Ed looked past my shoulder at the man standing behind me—moving beside me—and now he looked annoyed. "Aw, fuck," he said. "Luke Riggs."

So yeah, it was. And that was the story of my life right there: *Aw, fuck. Luke Riggs.*

"Remember me?" the voice said, and I almost turned and shouted at him, offended. But he wasn't talking to me; he was talking to Ed.

Ed's cheekbones went red, and he was glaring at Luke as hard as he could through his weed haze. "Sixth grade," he said. "You gave me a bloody nose and I had to spend an hour in the nurse's office. I was grounded for a week."

"So fucking easy," Luke said in that lazy drawl of his, like he had no rush to get the words out. His low voice hummed through my body, from my nipples straight down between my legs. "You practically walked into my fist. Like shooting fish in a barrel. I can do it again if you want."

Ed was silent, staring at him. Unbothered by the hostility, Luke reached past me and put a bottle of iced tea on the counter. I watched his arm—I knew that fucking arm, the ink, the magic tendons in his forearms, the flex of his biceps in a dark gray T-shirt—and I knew that hand. Oh yes, I knew it. Just the sight of it, the wide palm and the capable thumb and fingers, made me suppress a shiver. Even with one hand, Luke Riggs had always been able to get me off.

Over. And over. And over.

The hand disappeared, reappeared with some money in it. Dropped the money on the counter. And then Luke said, "Emily."

The breath left my throat. I turned my head and looked at him.

Oh, fuck. Luke Riggs.

Tall. Lean. Muscled. That familiar line of his jaw, shadowed dark with the beginning of a beard. Those cheekbones. That magic mouth, which had basically been my very favorite thing back in the day. Well, that and another part of Luke, not currently on display. I felt another shiver between my legs at the thought.

He was wearing a dark baseball cap, the brim pulled low over his eyes, but I could see his eyes in the shadows. I knew them, too. They were dark, they were quietly intense, and right now they were fixed on me.

It took a long second, caught by those eyes, before my brain stuttered back into some kind of action. We were standing in a gas station. Ed MacGregor was watching us, and the silence—and the stare—had gone on too long.

Oh yeah, and no one in town ever knew about Luke Riggs and me. Not ever.

I made myself clear my throat. "Luke," I said, my shitty impression of a casual greeting. "How are things?"

He didn't bother answering, just reached past me again—oh God, I could smell him, that familiar Luke Riggs smell, like citrus and hot, sweaty sex—and picked up his bottle of iced tea. "That your car on the side of the road back there?" he asked.

I had to pretend this was a normal conversation. That at eighteen I hadn't pressed my face in a pillow to muffle my screams of Luke Riggs' name before I woke up the neighborhood. "Car trouble," I croaked.

"Yeah," Luke said, "and no way to phone for help." His gaze flickered past me to Ed, and a smile touched his mouth. I knew that smile—it was Luke's *I win* smile. Everyone saw it when guys scrambled out of his way in the halls of Westlake High. Guys saw it when their girlfriends forgot their name when Luke was around. It was a smile that had started a lot of fights, all of which Luke won. "Looks like my lucky day," Luke said to Ed, "because you won't let a stranded woman make a phone call."

"What?" Ed said, startled. "Wait."

But Luke ignored him and looked at me. "I have a phone," he said, "and my car is out front. Which one do you want?"

"I, um." I couldn't speak, because in that second I was eighteen again, and we'd left Patty Dinsmore's house party and were making out in the trees behind her garage, and Luke's hand was between my legs, and his voice was low in my ear. *My cock or my tongue, Emily. Which one do you want?*

Luke's eyes on me were dark, and his smile was knowing. Because he was remembering exactly the same thing.

"Wait a minute," Ed MacGregor said. "She can use my phone. Emily, you can use my phone."

"She's not going to use your phone," Luke said.

I narrowed my eyes and thought about telling him off, because it was my decision. But then I remembered: I could either use Ed's phone and sit here for an hour, waiting for a tow truck and fending off Ed's clumsy advances, or I could walk out the door, get into Luke Riggs' car, and go.

It was no decision at all, really.

Shit.

"Fine." I snatched my purse up from the counter where I'd put it down and stared Luke right in the eye. "I need a ride, Luke. You think you can give me one?"

"Yeah," he said back. "I do."

I snorted. "We'll see." I wasn't going to give him that chance, dirty—very dirty—past or not. I wasn't eighteen anymore, and I'd sworn off men. Luke was a man. *Ergo*, there would be no riding. Whatsoever. "Let's go, then," I said, walking to the door. "Hurry up."

It was pretty good, as exits go.

I just hoped he'd follow me.

TWO

Luke

SHE WAS WORKED UP, I could tell. She was hot as hell, too, but that was Emily Parker.

She had that same hot body, those curves, those hips, that ass in jeans. That sexy tousled blonde hair. She was annoyed, sweaty, her shirt tied around her waist, her hair twisted back in a damp, messy, wind-blown ponytail. Her brows were drawn down over her dark-lashed gray eyes, her mouth—fuck, I'd done plenty with that mouth—was set in a firm line. Her movements were quick and harsh. Ed had annoyed her, and now I annoyed her. She was gorgeous, but this was Emily heading into full-on bitch mode.

Fuck, I loved bitch mode.

Eight years. Jesus. Eight freaking years. And now, today of all days, when I was finally taking the road back into town, here was Emily Parker. Like a welcome home present. *Hey, asshole, this is*

*what you could have had if you weren't who you are. If you
weren't Luke Riggs. If you were better.*

I followed her out the door—Ed was still protesting, which I
ignored—and into the parking lot. She'd stopped at the edge of
the concrete, staring at my car, her purse hitched over her shoulder. Emily might be a cop's daughter, one of the goody-two-shoes
Parker sisters, and far too good for me, but she'd always been able
to appreciate a nice car.

"Yeah," I said, walking past her, letting my shoulder brush
hers as I headed for the jet-black Dodge Charger. "That's mine."

It was her turn to follow me, which I heard her do. "Jesus,
Luke," she said. "Where the hell did you get that?"

"This particular car?" I thought back. "Omaha."

"When were you in Omaha?"

I beeped the doors unlocked and looked at her as I opened
the driver's door. "It's a long story," I said. "Eight years long."

She bit her lip, then circled around to the passenger side.
"I know."

I didn't have anything embarrassing in my car that I could
think of, even though I'd been on the road for days. No fast food
wrappers, because I didn't eat that shit. No condoms, because I
never fucked girls in my car. No other shit. There was a sweatshirt I'd tossed in the back seat, and a couple of my duffel bags in
the trunk, and that was it. Dad had drilled it into me and my
brothers since birth: You can treat your house like shit, you can
treat the people in your life like shit, but you always, always take
care of your car.

So Emily got in, settled back into the leather seat, and looked
around, and that was fine with me. She looked good there. She
did up her seat belt and did a little shiver as I started the engine,
and right then I wanted her. Wanted to put my hands on her, like
I had when we were eighteen. And man, I had had my hands
everywhere when we were eighteen. A dozen times. A hundred.

The two of us in secret, with no one ever knowing. Not her family, not my brothers. No one.

I'd had a vehicle back then, too. A pickup truck, a junker someone had left at Dad's shop in exchange for a few hundred bucks. I'd bought it off Dad and spent my spare time fixing it, making it run, and souping it up. That summer after high school finally ended, I'd spend my days working on my truck, and the nights I got lucky, a blonde named Emily would sneak into my bed and we'd fuck until dawn.

That had been a good summer. Until she left for college, and it was over. Because I was a Riggs, and I had no way of going to college, and we both knew it, while she was Emily Parker. She was a cop's daughter, destined for good things.

The breakup hadn't been messy or angsty, because it was always going to happen from the first. We had our hot, secret fun, and we both got off, until she packed her bags and left to start her actual life.

I hadn't seen her again until today.

"You want your stuff out of your car?" I asked her as I reversed out of the parking lot, my arm over the back of the seat.

She seemed to lean away from me, but I didn't take it personally. I'd caught her smelling me in the store a minute ago. "How do you know I have stuff in my car?" she said.

"Because every chick has stuff in her car."

Her eyebrows crashed down again. "God, you're an asshole," she said. "And yes, this *chick* has some things she needs to pick up."

I pulled out onto the highway and headed back the way I'd come, toward her car. "Don't leave anything valuable in it," I said. "Darren is reliable, but he tends to take shit if it's lying around."

"Excuse me?" Bitch mode on. "Who is Darren?"

"The tow truck guy who works for Dad's body shop," I said. "I'm calling him while you get your stuff."

"I can take care of this, Luke," she said. "Even though I'm a woman, and all. I didn't ask you to call a tow truck driver."

"No, but I'm calling one anyway," I said as we spotted her car and I did a U-turn on the empty road, pulling over behind it. "Because your phone is still dead, and I know Darren's number. I'm just that kind of guy."

"Believe me, I know exactly what kind of guy you are."

"Pretty much," I agreed. Emily was a lot of things, but stupid was never one of them. "You have five minutes," I said, pulling out my phone as she got out of the passenger seat. "Take too long, and your ride is taking off. You can go torture Ed to pass the time while you wait."

She had been about to slam the passenger door, but she turned and leaned in instead. "Leave me by the side of the road, and I am calling the *police*," she hissed. "Just try me, Luke Riggs." Then she slammed the door and walked ahead to her car.

Yeah, bitch mode still turned me on.

I called Darren while she thumped her bags into the back seat of my car—and no, I didn't help her. She'd made it clear that she could do it, being a woman and all. When Emily got like this, it was best to let her work it out. By the time she finished she was sweaty again, so I turned over the engine when she got in and turned up the air conditioning. "Iced tea?" I said, handing her my unopened bottle.

She took the bottle and downed the whole thing, then leaned back in the passenger seat as I pulled off the edge of the road. "Okay, I'm calm now," she declared. "What are you doing on this road, anyway?"

"Coming back to town," I said.

"From where?"

"Most recently, Florida. Before that, lots of places. I've been traveling around."

She seemed to think that over. "And why are you coming back now?" she asked.

"You really want to know?" I hesitated, but only for a second. Screw it. "Dad's in prison," I told her. I glanced at her from the corner of my eye, checking her reaction. "I know. Shocking, huh?"

Because it wasn't. Everyone—especially everyone in West-lake—always knew Mike Riggs would end up in prison. The only surprise was that it took so long.

But Emily bit her lip. "Jeez, Luke, I'm sorry," she said. "What —what is he in for?"

"He hit a guy with his car," I said. "He was half in the bag when he did it, and he was arguing with the guy, so it was sort of intentional. In the end he went down for attempted murder and impaired driving, so he'll be in for a while."

She was silent, not saying the words anyone else would say: *What do you expect from the Riggs family?* Westlake had an actual set of railroad tracks going through it, and we lived on the wrong side of them. Literally the wrong side of the tracks. Our mom had bailed on Dad, me, and my three brothers when I was four, leaving Dad to raise us alone. And Dad had done a shit job of it.

We'd run wild, my brothers and me. Fighting, stirring up trouble, doing whatever we wanted. We had no curfew, no one expecting us home to dinner, no one checking that we did our homework—or went to school at all. Dad ran a garage, where he mostly hung out, smoked weed, and shot the shit with his pothead buddies. When he remembered he had sons, it was usually to give one of us a few punches to the head—and then he'd ignored us again.

And no, we didn't call the cops when Dad belted us one. We didn't call Social Services or CPS or whoever the fuck. Because

Dad was bad, but whatever came after that phone call would be worse, and we all knew it.

In the meantime, we lived like stray cats. It didn't make us look good. That was why Emily, the precious daughter of one of Westlake's cops, should never have let me put my hands on her. She should never have gone near a Riggs boy at all.

But she had. For a little while, anyway.

THREE

Luke

"SO DAD IS out of the picture," I said conversationally, like this was my everyday reality and not something I should be fucking ashamed to admit. "The problem is, that leaves no one running the body shop. And the body shop makes a profit. So Dad got on one of those shitty prison phones and called me. It's my job, it turns out, to come home and keep the shop running, keep the money coming in."

"You?" Emily asked. "Not your brothers?"

I shook my head, stopping at a single light hanging from a wire overhead and taking a left toward town. "Let's say my brothers aren't available right now."

"Why not? Where did they go?"

"Well, let's see," I said. "Jace just got out of prison, and he's in a halfway house in Detroit."

She leaned forward, jerking against her seat belt, and stared at me. "Jace? *Jace* went to prison? Are you kidding me?"

"Surprise," I told her. Jace was the smartest of the four of us—which wasn't much of a competition, but still. Jace had always been the brother with the brains. The quiet one. "Grand theft auto. Did twenty months. He has to stay in the halfway house as a condition of his parole. So he can't come run the shop."

"Oh my God," Emily said. And for a second, even though the topic was my awful family life, I felt like I was settling in to something familiar. Emily may not like me—despite all the orgasms eight years ago—but she knew me. She knew my family. She'd grown up in the same place as all of us, gone to the same high school, hung out in the same spots, known the same people. It was a relief, in a way, not to have to explain myself like I would to a stranger. Strangers were all I had known for eight years.

She wasn't just familiar, she was Emily. I felt a weird ache, watching her and listening to her voice. But I pushed it away and let it go. I'd been letting go of that ache since the last time I saw her.

"Okay," Emily said, sitting back in her seat again. "Where's Ryan? Why can't he take over the shop? Don't tell me he's some big league baseball player."

I grinned at the road. "Don't follow sports much, huh?"

"I don't follow sports *at all*," Emily said. "You know that, Luke Riggs. So if Ryan is some famous athlete, I have no idea."

"He isn't," I said. This hurt too, another punch in the gut. Ryan was so fucking talented. "He made it to the minor leagues, but he got an injury three months ago. His shoulder. He's done, at least for now. Maybe forever."

"Oh," she said. "That's awful."

"Yeah, well, he also got in a fistfight with another player and broke his nose right in front of the crowd at a game, so he has other problems than his shoulder. He has to follow some kind of treatment, go to meetings or something, or his career is done. He also has a son to take care of."

"Ryan has a son?"

I nodded. "Dylan. He's seven. The mother is not in the picture. Ryan didn't even know Dylan existed until three years ago. It was one of those *Surprise, you have a son, see you later* situations."

"Jesus," Emily said. She sighed. "What about Dex? I think Mom said he's a cop."

"*Was* a cop," I corrected her. "He did four years on the Detroit PD. He resigned a year ago."

"Why?"

I tapped my fingers on the steering wheel. "That's a good question. The official line is that the stress was too much for him. The unofficial line is that there were potential charges of corruption coming down the pipe, so it was best to get out while he could do it clean. He's still in Detroit, doing private security work now."

Emily was quiet for a second, taking all of this in. "Okay, so he can't come help with the shop?"

"I asked him," I said. "His answer was *I'm never going back to that town, dipshit, so figure it out by yourself. I'd rather cut off my balls with a rusty saw.*"

She cleared her throat, part shock and part laugh. "That's vivid. But I have to admit I know how he feels." She glanced at me. "So it's true. You're the only one to take over the family business."

I lifted a hand from the wheel and touched it to the brim of my baseball cap in a salute. "Unemployed, unencumbered, and currently not incarcerated," I said. "So what are you doing on this road into town with a car full of luggage? I told you mine, now tell me yours."

I watched from the corner of my eye as she scrubbed a hand over her face. "I'm coming back," she said. "Like you are. But ugh, my problems are so stupid compared to yours."

"No one's problems are stupider than mine. Trust me."

She shook her head. "Mom is getting a career award, so there's this big thing happening on Friday. I have to be here for that."

"That sounds nice," I said. Emily's mother was a legend in Westlake, a woman cop who worked in the middle of a boys' club and never let anyone give her shit. I could say I admired her and actually mean it, but the Westlake PD and the Riggs family had always been on opposite sides. Of everything. I'd spent most of my life seeing cops as the enemy. And I'd long ago devirginized the sweet daughter of Westlake's most venerated cop.

I guessed Emily's mother wouldn't be an admirer of mine.

"She's happy but she's freaking out at the same time," Emily said. "She says it makes her feel old. And Lauren needs a break from running the hair salon for a while, so I got nominated."

I frowned to myself, trying to dredge up memories. I was pretty sure Emily's twin sister Lauren had gotten married pretty soon after high school. "You know how to run a hair salon?" I asked Emily.

"I have a business degree," she said, stiffening up straight in her seat. "I think I can handle it."

Of course. She'd gone to college. "A business degree," I said. "I always pictured you going off and being a big shot in some big company, wearing a skirt and heels every day."

"If you must know, I actually did that for a while. And yet here I am, coming back home in a broken-down car," she said. "You always knew how to make a girl feel good, Luke."

I always *did* know how to make a girl feel good. Especially her. "It's a compliment," I said.

"Really? It didn't sound like one. It sounded like you're pointing out what a failure I am."

I rolled my eyes. "You're right," I said. "You're in Westlake to see your mother and help your sister, so your life is over. You should just throw yourself off the Six Point bridge and end it now."

"You are such an asshole," she said, her voice rising. "I'm talking about my career being in the toilet here. Why did I ever put up with you eight years ago?"

"You know why," I said.

"Do not," she said, raising one index finger imperiously. "Do. *Not.* Bring that up. That did. *Not.* Happen."

I scratched a lazy thumb over my temple, just below the brim of my baseball cap. "Emily," I said slowly, like she was missing an important point. "It didn't happen, like, fifty times."

"I'm not listening," she said, taking that imperious index finger and pointing it at her ear, jabbing it. "I'm not. I can't hear you."

This was Emily in high school: smart, hot, and very fucking opinionated. The kind of girl sixteen-year-old guys didn't know what to do with, so behind her back they called her stuck-up and crazy. They said things like *She's hot, but she'd be hotter if she wasn't such a bitch.*

To her face, they didn't dare. They went after easier prey. Because they didn't know how to handle a girl so confident, so full of herself, that she didn't need their good opinion for two fucking seconds.

Me, I never understood that. Maybe it was my upbringing, but I never wanted soft and easy. I never wanted sweetness and light. I wanted a girl who could lose her shit and give me a tongue-lashing. It was fun then, and damn, it was fun now.

And I knew how to handle Emily. I had the secret. She may have been wild, but she always got sweet after I made her come.

Worked for me.

"Okay fine," I said, waving away her pointing finger like a fly. "We'll change the subject. You staying at your parents' place?"

"Yes," she said. "For now."

We had entered Westlake, and we were approaching Emily's neighborhood. Which, of course, was on the right side of the railroad tracks, so it was a neighborhood of well-kept middle-class houses, with nice gardens and big trees, where decent people lived.

In the seat next to me, I saw Emily stiffen, her body going tense. I glanced at her, at her profile staring straight ahead, and in that second I knew exactly what she was thinking. What had made her go from annoyed to suddenly self-conscious.

She was in my car, with me, and her family was going to see it.

It came as a surprise, the sting of that. I should have been used to it. Hell, if she'd asked me, I would have *told* her not to be seen with a Riggs brother. And still, that straight-ahead gaze, that set of her shoulders that said she was about to be embarrassed—I felt the blood go hot up the back of my neck.

Welcome home, Riggs. Good old Westlake.

This place never changed. Not in eight years. Not for a fucking second.

Well, fuck it.

"Just tell them I'm an Uber driver," I said as I drove up her street. There were cars in the driveway of her parents' house, which meant that at least one person was definitely home.

"It isn't that," she said, the words coming out of her mouth automatically, followed by a pause so long that I knew the words were a lie.

"Right," I said. I pulled to a stop next to the curb in front of her parents' house. There was no motion in the windows, but that didn't mean no one was looking. I opened my door and got out of the car.

Emily scrambled to follow, getting out as I opened the door to the back seat. "What are you doing?" she asked.

"Getting your bags," I said. I pulled them out one by one,

dropping them on the sidewalk. I didn't razz her about how heavy they were. I didn't say anything. The silence fell hard, like a fog. I watched from under the brim of my cap as she glanced uneasily between the house and the growing pile of her bags.

"Luke," she said finally, when I dropped the last bag on the pile.

Too little, too late. I already got the message. For a little while it had seemed like things might be different, that now we could act like normal people after all this time. But we couldn't. At least, she couldn't.

I shouldn't be in this neighborhood. I shouldn't be talking to Emily Parker, just like eight years ago. We were too far apart, and we always would be.

Fuck if I knew why that hurt, but it did.

So I shut down.

I closed the backseat door and leaned a hand on the roof of my Charger. "We're done," I told her. "Have a nice life."

"Luke," she said again.

"Tell them we ran into each other by chance. It's the truth. Maybe they'll believe it. And say hi to the Westlake PD for me."

She didn't answer. She just stood there, looking awkward and beautiful and maybe a little ashamed. But she didn't say anything else.

So I got in my car and drove off, leaving her standing on the sidewalk.

FOUR

Emily

I THOUGHT at first that there was no one in the living room when I walked into the house. The window overlooked the front yard and the sidewalk where Luke had dropped me off. I could hear voices at the back of the house, in the kitchen—Mom's and my sister Lauren's voices—but there was no one here.

Which meant no one had seen me get out of Luke's car. All of that stupidity on my part, acting like Luke was a case of leprosy I had to hide, for nothing.

I sighed and dropped my purse from my shoulder when a voice, soft and familiar, came from one of the living room chairs. "Emily."

I jumped and walked into the living room. Dad was sitting in one of the easy chairs, deeply ensconced in it, a folded-up newspaper on his knees. He had his half-glasses on and he was looking at me over their rims, his chin angled down, his thinning hair standing up on one side of his head like he'd brushed a hand through it and forgot about it.

I felt a rush of pure love, like I always did when I saw Dad. Mom was the cop in the family, and the one who got all the attention—she'd broken barriers in her career, she knew everyone in Westlake, and she'd often risked her life on the job. Mom, in short, was kind of glamorous. Dad worked at an insurance company, and Westlake saw him as the supportive husband who didn't mind taking a back seat to his wife. Dad didn't have fame or popularity, and he didn't have a high-risk job with crazy hours. In fact, with his nine-to-five office life, Dad had done a lot to raise Lauren and me, making our dinners and getting us to bed in the evenings when Mom wasn't home.

Dad was also quieter than Mom. He liked to read and putter around the house in his off hours. He and Mom made an odd couple, maybe, but they had made it work all my life.

"Dad," I said. "What are you doing sitting here alone?"

"Avoiding the kitchen argument," he replied. "I'm at the point where I wonder if I can sneak in and make myself a peanut butter and jelly sandwich without their noticing."

"Really?" Mom and Lauren never argued much. "What is it?"

"Just tension, I think." Dad shrugged. "It's supposed to be a special dinner, with you home and all of us together. It's mostly turned into a debate with no one winning."

I dropped onto the sofa opposite him. That was odd. We didn't have a lot of family arguments. It was also odd that Dad was sitting alone in the living room in the dark. "I'd be just as happy to order a pizza," I said.

"Me too." He gave me a brief smile, and he looked like Dad, but there was something different too. He looked drawn, like he hadn't been sleeping.

"How are you?" I asked him.

He surprised me by answering with a question. "Which Riggs boy was that?"

Oh. So he had seen. "Um. Luke."

"I see." I expected a lecture, but Dad sounded thoughtful. "Where is your car?"

"It broke down on the side of Road Six. Luke was passing by and gave me a ride home." It was nothing but the truth, and God, why had I gotten so worked up about my family seeing Luke drop me off? It was a ride. It wasn't like he'd stripped me naked in the family driveway. I felt an edge of guilt, thinking back to the look on Luke's face. His jaw tight, his eyes shuttered. *We're done.*

"That's very nice of him," Dad said. "Do you know that Mike Riggs is in prison for nearly killing someone?"

"Yeah, Luke mentioned that. He's in town to run the body shop while his dad is, um, gone."

"Mmm," Dad said, leaning back in his easy chair, his eyes still on me. He took off his half-glasses. "I see."

I rubbed my palms on my thighs, like I was eight again. "You see what?"

"I see that he left your luggage on the sidewalk, so the two of you aren't on good terms."

"I barely know him," I said, and God, why did that sound so awful coming out of my mouth? I'd had no problem lying about my relationship with Luke when we were eighteen. We'd barely crossed paths during the day, and at night we'd fucked like rabbits. I'd never thought twice about it. So why did I feel a little disgusted with myself right now? "Besides, I moved my own luggage in the door just fine. I'm not an invalid."

"Just be careful with the Riggs boys," Dad said. "They've been away, but with Mike in prison, no one is sure what they're going to do."

"What does that mean?"

Dad shook his head. "Just that it's smart to stay away from

them. And you've always been a smart girl. It's good to have you home, honey."

MOM AND LAUREN were in the kitchen, Mom at the sink, Lauren leaning against the fridge, her arms crossed. When I crossed the threshold, Mom dropped what she was doing and turned to me, opening her arms for a hug. "Emily!"

I stepped into her hold and let her hug me. Mom was a great mother, and very loving, but she was still a cop, and her grip was so hard it could crack ribs. "Mom, please," I gasped.

"Oh, stop. I'm just happy to have you home." She squeezed me again, making the breath come out of me. This was a little affectionate, even for Mom, and for some reason I got another uneasy feeling in my gut. Why was my mother clinging to me like she'd been worried?

Finally she let me go, then she patted my cheeks. Mom had left being a beat cop for the past ten years—she was now a sergeant, working mostly behind a desk—but she had never lost her fit policewoman physique. Even at fifty, with her hair in a braid down her back, she had strong arms and legs, a small bosom, and slim hips. I loved my mother, but there was no money in the world that would entice me to arm wrestle her. "You look beautiful," she said to me, stroking my hair. "Come have something to eat."

"Thanks." I glanced at Lauren. She was still leaning against the fridge, her arms crossed. "Hey, sis."

Lauren and I were twins—if you wanted to split hairs, she was two minutes older—but we were fraternal, not identical. Lauren's hair was a brownish honey-gold compared to my blonde, her eyes darker gray. She had slightly bigger boobs than me, which I knew because we'd measured them obsessively as teenagers.

Her hips were just slightly rounder than mine, my legs were an inch longer than hers, and our shoe size was identical. These are the things you know about your twin sister.

But I looked at her, and that unease turned in my gut again. She looked like Lauren, sure, but she looked different, too. Her face paler and devoid of makeup. Lauren had always been vain about her Jennifer Aniston hair in high school, but today it was in a sloppy half-up, half-down do, with tendrils hanging over her temples. She was wearing a threadbare sweatshirt with the UCLA logo on it, though Lauren had never been anywhere UCLA in her life.

"You made it," she said, picking up a crumpled piece of wax paper from the counter and tossing it at me, hitting me square in the forehead. "Like, finally."

We weren't demonstrative, Lauren and me. Maybe it was because we'd literally shared a uterus. We always felt we were close enough without doing the hugging thing. "I made it," I said.

Lauren's eyes narrowed. "We're deciding on dinner," she said, "or trying to. I want to cook, but Mom says no. Great vote of confidence, huh?"

"It isn't that," Mom said. "I just don't think you need to do all the cooking tonight."

"You're getting a big award, Mom," Lauren said. "So you think you should be the one to do all the work?"

"No, I just think—"

"Dad and I vote for pizza," I said.

They both gave me a funny look—I had no idea why— and then Lauren said, "No pizza. I told you, I can cook."

"And I told you, you don't have to do all the work," Mom said.

I ducked behind Mom and stole some of the vegetables she was chopping on the counter, because I was starving. My alarms were up. Mom and Lauren always got along; I was the one who had the big drama, the blowups growing up. *You don't love me! My life is awful!* Yeah, I'd been a treat at fourteen, while Lauren sat in her room and did her homework. Lauren never made a fuss.

Even when she'd asked me for help, she'd done it in an understated text. *I need some help running the salon. I'm doing sixteen-hour days and it's too much. Do you think you can come and pitch in?*

Something wasn't right. Dad alone in the living room, Mom and Lauren arguing, Lauren looking washed out. I'd been away too long. What the hell was happening?

I excused myself from the kitchen to bring my bags up to my room. My childhood room. Which had the same single bed in it I'd had as a teenager, though at least Mom had updated it with new sheets and a dark blue comforter, and my teenage crush posters had been taken down from the walls.

As I was dropping the last suitcase in the corner, Lauren appeared in the doorway, looking around. Her lips curled and her eyebrows went up in the first sign of real amusement I'd seen on her face.

"Nice," she teased. "You're gonna see a lot of action in here, Emily."

"Ugh, shut up," I said. "It's temporary."

"I'd put you up at our house, but Vic..." She trailed off. "Our guest room is full of junk right now."

"It's fine," I said. Vic, Lauren's husband, wasn't keen on entertaining. He was the quiet type, like her. I'd never really known what Lauren saw in him. I'd always gone for the popular guys in high school, the flashy guys. At least, I had until I made out with Luke Riggs one night during a big football game, then given it up to him three weeks later. Luke was hot, and he was notorious, but he wasn't the popular type at all.

Since I'd left for college, I'd gone back to my old pattern:

good-looking guys, outgoing guys, popular guys. Football players. That was what I knew; that was the kind of guy I was supposed to be with. Outgoing hot blonde plus outgoing hot guy equals perfection. Except I ended up so frustrated I swore off men forever.

I stretched my aching back and looked at my sister, pushing away my feelings of failure. "So what's going on?" I asked her.

For a second she almost looked panicked. "What do you mean?"

"Something's wrong," I said. "Something's weird."

"Emily, nothing is weird." She sounded exasperated, like I was a toddler. "Everything is fine. It's all in your head."

I bit back a retort. Now was not the time for a shouting match, I guessed. "Fine. Do you want to talk?"

"What about?"

I couldn't say *You look freaking terrible*, so I said, "The salon."

"Not now." She rubbed her fingertips over her forehead. "Come by tomorrow and I'll show you the ropes. We open at ten, so come at nine."

"Okay." Now I was trying not to panic. *You're being dramatic, Emily.* "You know I can't cut hair, right?"

"I don't need you to cut hair. I have stylists for that. It's the other stuff that's killing me. Accounting, bookkeeping, marketing. That kind of thing."

"I can do that."

"I just want..." Lauren looked frustrated through her exhaustion. "I just want an afternoon off. God, a day. A whole day."

"You can take a day," I said to her. "You can take a whole week. I'll do all of it for you."

She sighed. "Let's just take it one step at a time, all right? Just start with a couple of things."

Right. Blonde, dramatic Emily had to be eased into things so she wouldn't explode. A contrast to steady Lauren, with her husband and her business. Lauren was the grownup, while I was the child. Even though I now had a college degree.

My jaw was aching, but I kept my mouth shut. "Nine o'clock tomorrow," I said. "I'll have to get up at seven to get my chance at the bathroom."

For a second she almost smiled—our house had only one bathroom, and the battles for it had been legendary when there were twin teen girls in the house. She didn't live here anymore, but she got the joke. Then she quirked one perfectly arched eyebrow.

"Luke Riggs?" she said.

My jaw dropped open. "What?"

"Luke Riggs," she said again. At the expression that must have been on my face, she finally gave me her first real smile. "You think I didn't see? You're so busted."

"He gave me a ride," I said. "That's it."

"Uh huh. Because Luke Riggs is just nice like that."

"It was innocent!" I protested.

"Suuuure." Lauren made the word draw out, like we always did when we were teasing each other about boys. "You think he'll like this room?" she asked, looking around my pathetic bedroom again. "I guess you can tell Mom and Dad you're helping him with his homework, but I don't think they'll believe you."

I flopped back on the bed. "You are so full of shit," I said. "I'm a grown woman. I can get a ride from whoever I want."

But she gave me that knowing, twin-sister grin, and left the room, closing the door behind her.

I stared at the ceiling.

"Damn," I said.

FIVE

Luke

TWO DAYS after I'd left her standing next to a pile of her luggage on the sidewalk, I stood under Emily Parker's Tercel, which was up on a hoist at Riggs Auto. One of my mechanics, Ted, had just finished going over it with me. "Transmission's done for," Ted said. "Brake pads, oil, no fluids, tires are bald. Bottom line, this car is pretty fucked."

I scratched my chin. He was right—I could see it myself, since Dad had taught all of us how to fix a car since sometime around first grade. "How did she drive this piece of shit for so long?" I said.

"Chicks, man," Ted said. "They're hopeless with this shit. I hear she's a dumb blonde."

I turned and looked at him for so long that he finally looked away. "I hope you don't say that shit in front of customers. No wonder we never get women in here."

"We get plenty of women," Ted said. He pointed, grinning. "They're right over there."

I followed his point to a stack of magazines piled on an old cabinet in the corner. "*Hustler?*" I said. "We have fucking *Hustler?* What is it, 1975?"

Ted shrugged. "Mike liked them. That's how we did things when Mike was here."

I'd been hearing that a lot since I'd been back. I'd spent time at my dad's body shop growing up—we all had. My brothers and I had learned how to fix cars from an early age, and we learned it by coming to Riggs Auto and getting dirty. We knew the guys who worked for Dad, the customers who came and went. Riggs Auto wasn't exactly a happy place, but it had been normal enough.

Something had changed. The guys working here now hadn't been here eight years ago. These guys were lazy and pissy, I wouldn't trust any of them with my wallet, and they seemed to make a game of trying to piss me off. I was the new guy, Mike's kid, the one they didn't trust, so I spent half my day looking over everyone's shoulder and making them even moodier.

We didn't have any customer service to speak of, which meant we didn't have all that many customers. I wondered why Dad said I had to come and run the shop so I could keep the profit coming in. What profit?

"Do the repairs," I said to Ted.

"Yeah?" Ted said. "Is blondie gonna pay?"

"You told a customer to fuck off yesterday," I said. "Suddenly you care about money?"

He laughed at that. "Sure, I care about money."

I didn't like the sound of that laugh. In the last two days I'd stared at invoices and waybills, trying to add up sales tax and payroll. Riggs Auto was run on scraps of paper and wads of cash instead of complicated computer programs. The scraps of paper had Dad's illegible handwriting on them and the bank account was barely used, yet none of the guys were complaining about missed pay. The whole thing stunk, and even a dumbass like me could see that the IRS would have a heyday in here.

Then there was the house.

Our place on the wrong side of Westlake's tracks was a mess. It sat on half an acre of overgrown weeds, and once upon a time— a hundred years ago, maybe—it had been a home for a family with money. The house itself was big, with a wraparound porch and four huge bedrooms. There was also a guest house set behind the main house, its own separate little place with a bedroom and bathroom. I'd lived in the guest house growing up, which made it easy for Emily to sneak into my bed every night without anyone seeing. That last summer, the guest house had probably seen more action than a porn theater in 1970s Times Square.

But my brothers and I hadn't exactly been big on upkeep, and since we all bailed, Dad had let the place fall to pieces. The paint was peeling, the shingles were curling, and the weeds were past my knees in June. When I wasn't wading through the mess at Riggs Auto during the day, I spent my evenings trying to at least make the main bedroom and the kitchen more habitable so I wasn't creeped out by my own house. Washing sheets, dishes, curtains, and floors was not what I was used to doing, and both nights I'd fallen into bed exhausted.

But I'd still been thinking about Emily. Because apparently the minute I got within Westlake city limits, she was the main thing on my mind. Even after she treated me like dirt on her shoe.

"Fix it," I said to Tom again, indicating her screwed-up car.

The car was her problem. I shouldn't fix it. I'd told her we were done. I should give her the number for a tow truck driver and send her on her way. She should get her car fixed on the right side of the tracks, far away from me, the guy she didn't want to be seen with. And yet, here I was.

Shit.

I walked back to the front office, which was empty. The phone on the front desk was ringing—for God knew how long, because none of the guys ever answered it—so I picked it up. "Riggs Auto."

"Jesus, Luke. Dad hire you as the receptionist?"

I felt a headache somewhere in the back of my head. It was my brother Ryan, calling from his place in the Detroit suburbs. "What do you want?" I asked him.

"Checking in on the family business," he said.

"Not your business," I said. "Your business is baseball."

Or it had been. Ryan's baseball career had been stalled by a bad shoulder, and no one knew if it would ever get back on track. In the meantime Ryan lived in his suburban house with his seven-year-old son and did... I had no idea what he did. Moped, maybe. My brothers' emotional states weren't my top priority, and mine wasn't theirs. We'd grown up in the same house, that was all. Roommates more than brothers. We'd never even liked each other all that much.

"If it turns out I'm a has-been," Ryan said, "then my business will be Riggs Auto."

"Yeah? You gonna come out here to Westlake and fix cars?"

"If I do, are you gonna stop me?"

"No," I said. "We need someone to clean the bathrooms. And you're right, we could use a receptionist."

"Dad goes to prison and suddenly you're a CEO," Ryan said. "It's like your IQ jumped overnight. From zero to thirty."

If you can believe it, Ryan was actually one of my nicer brothers. "Did you call for a reason, or just to bust my balls?"

"I called for a reason." In the background, I heard Dylan's voice. "Hold on," Ryan said to his son. "I'll be done in a sec."

It was the middle of a weekday. "Shouldn't he be in school?" I asked Ryan.

"Yeah. He told me he was sick this morning, but now I think he was full of shit."

"You just said *shit* in front of a seven-year-old," I pointed out.

"I did," Ryan said, "and here it is in another sentence: You don't know shit about parenting."

"You know what?" I said. "I just decided I'm glad you called. Maybe you can tell me what the hell Dad is up to."

"Right now?" Ryan said. "Let's see. He probably just finished a terrible prison meal and is going back to his cell to watch TV."

"You know what I mean, dipshit. I mean Riggs Auto. These guys Dad hired. The fact that there's no money in the bank and no customers, yet everyone is paid. The fact that there are no records and the safe is empty, yet there are no creditors calling."

Ryan was quiet.

"I'm dumb, but I'm not that dumb," I said. "If you have something to tell me, say it."

"Okay, well," Ryan said. "That's the reason I'm calling. It's sort of possible that there are a few illegal things going on at the body shop."

Possible? A few? I felt my stomach sink. "I'm waiting for you to say more," I prompted.

"I'm not involved," Ryan said. "None of us are. We barely talk to Dad anyway, but he's been extra cagey the last few years. He cleaned out his employees and brought in a bunch of dirtbags. And the place has no customers, but he's suddenly had a bunch of money to throw around."

I ran a hand through my hair. It all clicked together. Jesus, how fucking dumb could Dad be? "Stolen cars," I said. "He's been doing chop shop work. It must be."

"I don't know," Ryan said. "I'm serious. But I got a phone call from Dad's lawyer today. We've been summoned to the bank."

"Summoned to the bank?" I said.

"Apparently there's a safe deposit box at the bank that we're supposed to go open. Dad's instructions. The lawyer doesn't know anything else. We're supposed to be there Friday at two."

The front door of the shop opened, and Emily Parker walked in. She paused, looking around—probably for me.

"This makes no sense," I said to Ryan, my eyes on Emily. "Dad has never had a safe deposit box in his life. What the hell is in it?"

"We probably don't want to know, but we have no choice."

Damn. Emily stood out like a sore thumb in the body shop, and some of Dad's dirtbags had noticed her. "Friday at two," I said to Ryan. "I'll be there. Call the others. I gotta go." I hung up and left the front desk, heading toward Emily as she turned and saw me.

She was wearing jeans, a white T-shirt, and a pair of flip-flops. She had a little bit of makeup on her face and her blonde hair was down over her shoulders. And even though I was mad at her, she was the sexiest fucking woman I had ever seen.

Maybe it was because I knew what her body looked like under the clothes—or at least I used to know. She was all curves, planes, and flawless skin, her nipples dark pink against white, and I'd had my hands over every inch of it. My tongue, too. It didn't matter what Emily wore, or how many years had gone by—to me, she always looked naked. Even when she was looking down her privileged nose at me.

Her gaze flicked down over me and back up again as I walked toward her. It was quick, but she had just checked me out. I tried not to grin as her expression grew annoyed. "Hey," she said as I approached. "You said you'd get my car. Where is it?"

I pulled a cloth from my back pocket and wiped my hands with it, slower than I needed to, rubbing at the caked-in grease. "It's in the back," I told her.

"Okay," she said. "Can I have it back?"

"No, because it doesn't run."

She looked stricken. "At all?"

"Was it running when I picked you up from the side of the road the other day?"

She blew out a breath. "Are you being difficult because of what happened in front of my house?"

"You mean when you were a dick to me?"

"Women can't be dicks."

"You proved otherwise."

She looked mad and guilty at the same time. No one could whip up a soup of emotion like Emily Parker. "I *may* have been out of line," she said.

I put the rag back in my pocket. "Looks like I got some spare Tercel parts. Have a nice day."

"Okay, okay." She bit her lip, ran a hand through her hair. Always a drama queen. "I apologize, Luke," she said, the words slow. "You helped me out and gave me a ride, and I was rude to you. In fact, I was a bit of a bitch." She emphasized that last word and glared at me.

Only Emily would imply that I was *supposed* to call her a bitch. "I suppose I accept," I said, "but your car is in bad shape. That's the truth."

"Can I see it?"

I shrugged. "Sure," I said. "Though you won't know what you're looking at."

She put her hands on her hips, which made her breasts look even nicer under the T-shirt. "Maybe I will know. Maybe I learned about cars."

I just stared at her, my eyebrows raised. She broke first.

"Shit," she said. "Fine. But I still want to see it."

"All right, Emily," I said. "Let's go."

SIX

Emily

I WAS DOING everything all wrong. I was supposed to walk into Riggs Auto, all cool and collected. I was supposed to calmly apologize to Luke for the way I'd treated him the other day, like a civilized person. I was supposed to collect my car. And then I was supposed to leave.

None of that was happening, and it was my fault. I was being Crazy Lady again, and I knew why. It was his stupid sexy body, his gorgeous arms with the ink on the right one, his gorgeous face with the high cheekbones and the dark eyes. He wasn't wearing a baseball cap today, and his black hair was tousled. There was a dark shadow on his jaw like he hadn't shaved in a day or two. Even his hands were hot—big and capable with a few faint smears of grease on the backs of the fingers. His *hands*. I was such an idiot.

He led me back to the bays where the cars were—ugh, God,

his ass in jeans was just as amazing as it had been at eighteen—
and pointed to my car, which was up on a hoist. "There," he said
in his low drawl. "Now you've seen it."

I crossed my arms and stared up at the underside of my car,
unwilling to admit that this was a pointless exercise, even though
he already knew. "It looks fine to me," I said, faking it. "I don't see
the problem."

"Yeah?" I turned to see Luke leaning one hip on a stack of
boxes, watching me stare up at my car. His expression was calm
and slightly amused, though it was still closed off. I wondered if
that meant he was still angry. "Is that your expert opinion?"
he said.

Past his shoulder, I could see one of the other mechanics in
the shop watching us. "Okay, fine," I said to Luke. "I admit I don't
know what the underside of my car is supposed to look like. But I
can't have you fix it, because I can't afford it."

That made Luke frown. "How are you going to get around?"
he asked.

"I borrowed Lauren's car," I said. "I can work something out
with her, maybe. Or my parents might lend me theirs."

"And then what? You get a new car? You have the money
for that?"

"It doesn't matter, because I don't have the money for this." I
pointed to my car.

"You do if I don't charge you for the repair."

I stared at him. It was completely unexpected, and for some
reason that made my defenses go up. "You're not going to charge
me? For a repair this expensive?"

"No."

"Why not?" I said. "What do you want instead?"

As soon as the words were out of my mouth, I knew they
were stupid. Stupid, and—this sounds weird—unworthy. Luke

and I had a lot of history, most of it dirty, but never, even at eigh-teen, had he treated sex as a transaction. No matter how hot and heavy we got, sex had always been something we did together for fun.

It made him mad again. I could see it. We'd had exactly two interactions since we'd both come back to town, and both times I'd made him mad. *Two for two, Emily.* I didn't know why I couldn't stop treating Luke like he was something he wasn't. Like I'd never met him before. Like I didn't trust him.

He slapped the palm of his hand on the box he was leaning on and stood up straight. "We'll discuss this in the office," he said, his jaw tight.

He headed across the garage to a door in the back. The mechanic was still watching us—actually, now everyone in here was watching us, and I'm not going to lie, these guys were kind of creepy. I followed Luke to the door, my cheeks going red.

When he shut the door behind us, he turned on me. "Jesus, Emily," he said. "I'm trying to do something fucking nice here."

We were in a small office, furnished with only a desk, covered in papers, and a chair. There wasn't even a computer on the desk. "I know," I said to him. "I shouldn't have said that. There's some-thing seriously wrong with me."

He watched me with narrowed eyes, like he suspected a trap.

For some reason, that was the worst thing—that he looked at me like that. No matter what drama I inflicted on him, Luke usually looked at me with quiet amusement, lazy indifference, or flat-out lust. Not like he thought I was going to kick him in the nuts without warning.

"I'm stressed out," I said. "I'm back in Westlake because I have no job and nowhere else to be. My last job was an internship that paid peanuts. I'm literally living in my childhood bedroom, sleeping in a single bed, with my parents in the bedroom next door—and I'm *twenty-six*. There's something wrong with Lauren, and she won't talk to me about it. I've spent two days in a hair salon, trying to figure out Lauren's business and inhaling hair spray. I'm getting rides because my car is fucked and I have no money to fix it. And apparently I've decided to take all of it out on you."

He crossed his arms. He was wearing a black T-shirt and jeans. God help me, Luke Riggs in a black T-shirt and jeans was the best thing I'd seen in seven long, sworn-off-men months, though I hated to admit it. "That it?" he said, his voice still curt. "Are you done?"

"Dumping on you?" I said. "I hope so. I mean, I know you have your own problems, because you're running a business all of a sudden and your dad is in prison. And on top of all that, you're trying to do something nice for me."

"Trying," he said with a poker face.

"I'll pay you," I said.

"Do not fucking pay me."

I ignored him and pulled out my wallet. I knew I had exactly one hundred dollars in it, mostly in fives and tens—money I had planned to buy groceries with, since I was mooching my parents' food. Instead I pulled out the bills and put them on the desk.

Luke looked at the bills, his dark eyes swiftly counting them. "A hundred bucks?"

"It's a down payment."

Now he sounded like he was getting mad again. "Christ, have you always been this stubborn? I'm trying to remember, but all I can recall is you moaning in my ear."

"I do not moan," I said.

His eyebrows went up, because that was a flat-out lie and we both knew it. With him, I had moaned. A lot. In fact, we'd never argued at eighteen—we'd only fucked. We had the same thought at the same time, and for a second the room was silent, the temperature between us going up and up.

"How long since you swore off men, Parker?" he said.

For a second I thought he was psychic, but then I remembered he'd heard me tell Ed MacGregor this at the gas station.

"Or was that a line?" Luke said.

"It wasn't a line," I snapped.

"Then how long?"

"Seven months." Because apparently I was an idiot who answered all of Luke's personal questions.

He shook his head in pity. "Seven months without dick. I know you, Em. You can barely go seven days."

"That isn't true." It had only been true with him, which I would not admit under pain of torture right now. "I get along just fine, believe me. I'm much happier. I don't need *dick*, as you put it."

His voice went down a notch. "It always sounds dirtier when you say it."

Was that a come-on? My brain didn't know, but my body gave a little throb of excitement, focused right between my legs. It was a familiar refrain pulsing through my blood: *Luke Riggs! Yes please! Right here! Right now!* But no. That was not happening. Even though eighteen-year-old Emily would have pushed down her jeans and hopped up on the desk and—no.

I cleared my throat, surprised I was still able to see through the testosterone haze in the room. "My car," I said, trying to sound businesslike, though my voice came out low and throaty, like a lounge singer's.

"Will be fixed," Luke said, finishing my sentence. "You want to give me your hundred bucks, fine, I'll take your hundred bucks. We'll work out the rest."

"Okay," I said. "Thank you."

"You got a number?" he said. "I'll call you when it's done."

So I gave him my number, and he texted me one word—*hi*—to give me his.

I had his number now, but I wasn't going to use it. Business only.

That was what I told myself when I walked out the door.

SEVEN

Luke

IF YOU WERE GOING to reunite the four Riggs brothers for the first time in eight years, Detroit was probably the place to do it. Down-and-out Detroit, which was still fighting and giving off attitude after the rest of the country had written it off. Dex had been a cop here; Ryan had played minor league baseball in Plymouth; Jace was in a halfway house here. I'd stayed here a few times during my nonstop wandering, never quite able to stay away. I liked the food and the music and the women. We were born in Westlake, but Detroit was a Riggs home away from home.

I picked up Jace at his halfway house. It was only when Jace told me he planned to take the bus across town to the bank that I found out he didn't have a car. "I think Dad sold it while I was in," Jace told me calmly on the phone. "I just take the bus now."

A Riggs without a car—any kind of car, even a junker—was like a Riggs without a dick, and we both knew it. I didn't rub it in, though, because after twenty months in prison, Jace had been through enough.

I found the halfway house, and my stomach sank. It was a shitty, boxy building, a 1980s brick square of apartments on a rundown street a few blocks from the community center. A woman, rail-thin and tired, sat on the front step smoking a cigarette.

I wasn't a stranger to people who were down and out. Whatever money the body shop made, Dad kept it, and my brothers and I lived off of whatever cash we could lift from his wallet. I'd had days when I went to school hungry, and so had my brothers. So to me, being on the down side of life wasn't something to be ashamed of; it was just something that happened to some of us. The first thing being poor teaches you is that it has nothing to do with whether you're a good person or a bad one.

Still, it bothered the fuck out of me, seeing Jace live in a place like this. Because even though Dex was the cop and Ryan was the ball player, Jace was the best of us—he just didn't get any credit for it. He was the quiet one, the brother who sat in the back of the classroom not because he was stupid, but because he was so smart he was bored as hell. He was the brother who stole books from the library while Dex stole cigarettes. Teachers assumed he cheated when his marks were good, because he was a Riggs, so he stopped bothering. Other kids picked fights with him, but it was always Jace who got suspended from school.

Dad gave Dex the most hits—Dad and Dex were like oil and water, with Dex giving the hits back when he got big enough—but Dad pretended Jace didn't exist at all, like he had never happened. At home, Jace was a shadow. After high school he worked at Riggs Auto for a while, then moved to Detroit where he got a job at another garage. We thought he had at least settled down to a quiet life, which was why we were all surprised as hell when he was arrested for stealing cars. His specialty was getting into parked cars and he'd never hurt anyone, but Jace pleaded guilty and he went down for twenty months, his life spiraled away down the drain.

He came out the front door of the halfway house now, wearing jeans, motorcycle boots, and a worn grey T-shirt under a short-sleeved black button-down worn open. I could see the ink on both his biceps, the trail of it down the inside of his left forearm. His dark hair was cut close to his head at the sides, his beard trim. He had lost weight inside and was packed with lean muscle, not much bulk, but he was tall, wide-shouldered, long-legged. He looked lethal and he moved quick. Anyone coming across Jace in a dark alley would turn and go the other way, with no idea that he was probably thinking about some book he read and not about mugging you at all.

"Hey," he said when he got in the passenger side. "Thanks for the ride."

"I'm getting you a car," I told him, reversing out of the lot.

"No point," Jace said. "Someone around here will just steal it."

I pulled out into traffic. If Jace thought that was an ironic statement, he didn't say so. "How much longer do you have to stay there?"

"Three weeks," he said, looking out the passenger window at the city going by. "Condition of parole. I got a mechanic's job at the garage a few blocks away—he takes most of the ex-cons. Not much money, but my PO does random checks to make sure I'm where I'm supposed to be, make sure I'm at work, make sure I'm clean. I pass the checks, I can move out."

I frowned. "Make sure you're clean?" I asked.

He smiled his quiet Jace smile at me, then he looked out the window again. "Standard procedure, Luke," he said. "Imbibing chemicals has never been my thing. Most evenings my PO finds me sitting in my apartment reading a book. I think he thinks I'm fooling him somehow, even though I piss in as many cups as he tells me to. Even when he watches."

Jesus. I was mad that Jace had to live with this kind of humiliation, and at the same time I couldn't reconcile the brother I knew with a man who would spend his time stealing cars. Who the hell had that guy been, and what was wrong with him?

"Come live at the house when you're out," I told him. "You can have the guest house. We'll find you a junker behind the body shop and you can at least get around. And you have a job, too."

Jace was quiet for a long minute, his gaze still fixed out the window. He slowly scratched his beard with fingers even more grease-stained than mine. "You sure you want a felon around?" he asked.

"I don't know," I said, my voice coming out more harsh than I intended. "Are you gonna fuck me over?"

"Maybe," Jace said, surprising me. "You don't really know."

"Cut the shit, Jace," I said.

"Fine," he said. "I'll think about it."

It made him sound like he had so many important places he could go instead, but I understood it. This was classic Riggs. We hate to admit we're in a bind, we hate to take help—especially from each other—and we hate to say thank you. It comes from being assholes, but it also comes from being sure that whatever good thing is being offered to you either comes with a catch or an expiry date. From being sure that even if someone is being nice to you, a minute from now they'll stop and you'll be on your own again.

When Mike Riggs is your father, these are the earliest life lessons you learn.

"This thing of Dad's," I said, changing the subject, "this safe deposit box. You have any idea what's in it?"

Jace shook his head. "I don't talk to Dad much. He's never said anything about it to me."

"What about the guy Dad tried to run over?" I asked. "You know him?"

"Ron Ruvinsky," Jace said. "You've met him. He calls himself Ronny Red."

"Ronny Red?" I said, shocked. Ronny had hung around the body shop from time to time when we were teenagers, getting drunk with Dad. "Dad tried to kill Ronny Red? Why?"

Jace shrugged. "I guess they got in an argument."

I ran a hand through my hair. Well, it was too late now. For whatever reason, Dad had tried to run over Ronny while drunk, and now he was paying for it.

"You were away a long time," Jace said. "You missed some things."

"You left too," I pointed out.

"We all did," Jace agreed. "We wanted to get the hell out of Westlake, away from Dad. But none of us went very far, except you. And we're all back here, so it didn't work."

"Don't remind me," I said. "I'm the one at Riggs Auto, trying to figure out a pile of Dad's receipts."

"Be careful," Jace said, and for a second his voice was cold. "Dad got into some bad shit in the last few years."

I stopped at a red light and stared at him. Before I could ask him what he meant, the light changed and Jace spoke again. "I always envied you," he said.

I blinked. "What?"

"Getting away," he explained. "We all talked about it, thought about it, but you just got in your car and went. Put your foot on the gas and didn't take it off." He shook his head. "You made it look so easy."

It felt like a gut punch for some reason. I didn't know why, but I didn't want my brother to have a fake idea of what my life had been like. "It wasn't that easy," I said, trying to explain. "There were a lot of times it was hard. Like anything else, I guess."

"Yeah, but when it got hard, you just packed your bags and kept going," Jace said. His voice had a wistful note to it. Any guy doing twenty months in a cell would fantasize about getting in a car and driving, not looking back.

Still. "You can pack your bags and keep going," I told Jace honestly, "but you're still carrying your shit around with you wherever you go. You're still you. Except you're carrying all of your shit in a crowd of strangers." I shrugged. "To tell the truth, I saw a lot of great things, a lot of great places. But most of it was lonely."

It was a weird confession, and I didn't know why I made it.

But Jace just nodded.

"Yeah," he said, looking out the window again. "I know that feeling."

THE BANK WAS off Rosa Parks, down near West Riverfront Park. I parked the Charger, next to a big, showy black SUV—that was definitely Ryan's—and a dark green Impala with dented fenders that was most likely Dex's. I got out, inhaling the smell of dirty water and motor oil, taking in the exotic sight of a closed, boarded-up hotel and a CVS. "This looks like Dad's kind of place," I said.

"Swank," Jace agreed, getting out of the passenger side.

Ryan and Dex were standing by the front doors, Ryan leaning against the wall with his hands in the pockets of his jeans, Dex standing with his feet apart and a smoke in his hand. They seemed to be facing off.

This wasn't new. Ryan and Dex had never gotten along,

mostly because they were only four months apart. No, our mother wasn't a biological wonder—Ryan had a different mother, and the same father, as the rest of us. In short, Dad had knocked up Mom four months before he'd knocked up another woman on the side. Mom produced Dex, and the other woman produced Ryan.

There was a reason the good people of Westlake stayed on the other side of the tracks.

Eventually both women bailed—no woman hangs around the Riggs men for long—and Dad ended up with both sons, plus me and Jace by then. It was like the Brady Bunch, except with cheating and a group of boys who didn't like each other. Ryan and Dex were particularly toxic, maybe because of their mothers, maybe because they were so close in age, and maybe just because they couldn't fucking get along.

"Thank God the cavalry is here," Ryan said as he saw Jace and me approaching. "Someone else deal with this asshole." He jerked a thumb at Dex.

Ryan, damn him, was probably the best-looking Riggs brother, if you liked the movie-star type. He had dark eyes and thick dark hair—carefully tousled—and he'd been born with a sensitive, soulful look on his face, like he was quietly pondering a deep line of poetry instead of thinking the dirty shit he was really thinking. He'd also been born with an athlete's grace and a throwing arm that set him apart from every other kid in Westlake. The whole package made girls fall for him in droves, so it was easy to hate Ryan for a while.

But Ryan was his own worst enemy, getting into fights and pissing off coaches, stalling his would-be career. Three years ago a woman had left him with a four-year-old son he didn't know he had—he'd knocked her up in a one-night stand at twenty. Then his shoulder had put a stop to his career. Today he was clean-shaven, wearing a pair of aviator shades, faded jeans, and a brown leather jacket over a white T-shirt. He was leaning against the wall near the door, and a woman coming out of the bank just about fell down the steps as she stared at him. He didn't notice.

Dex looked rougher, like he had just gotten out of bed, which he probably had. His old jeans were low-slung and the blue plaid button-down he had pulled on was on its fourth or fifth straight wear. He had a four-days' beard and a half-crazy look in his eyes I recognized from childhood. Dex was the oldest, the first Riggs to terrorize the schools and the neighborhood, and Dex was the craziest. He was the one who took dares to jump off roofs or stand in the middle of train tracks. He was the one who could shoplift like a pro when he wanted to and somehow get liquor when he was fifteen. His teachers practically had to get PTSD counseling, and guidance counselors despaired.

The fact that Dex ended up as a cop surprised everyone, but it didn't surprise Jace, Ryan, or me. Dex didn't become a cop because he wanted to serve and protect—he did it because just the thought of it made Dad furious. Dex may have been crazy, but when he set his mind to something he could always do it—and there was nothing he set his mind to more than making Dad miserable. Dex hated Dad more than he hated anyone.

"Listen, dipshit," he said to Ryan, "I didn't ask to be here any more than you did. So let's just get this over with."

"Is that a joint?" I asked Dex, catching the smell of his smoke. "Jesus, man, this is a bank. Put that out."

"I need something to take the edge off," Dex said, taking another toke. "This is going to suck."

He was probably right about that. I was dreading whatever Dad had left us in this safe deposit box, and from the looks on my brothers' faces, they did too.

"Luke the wanderer," Ryan said, looking me over from his position leaning against the wall. "How's Westlake?"

"It still sucks, thanks," I told him.

"Any of the hot girls from high school still there?" he asked.

It was an uncanny question, like he could reach into my brain and see Emily Parker, but of course he didn't know anything about me and Emily. Not that there was anything to know anymore, except for my dirty thoughts. "A few," I said.

"So it isn't all bad, then," Ryan said, grinning.

"As if you'd have a shot," Dex said to Ryan, dropping his joint and grinding it out with his toe. "Women don't like package deals."

Ryan looked Dex up and down, like he'd looked at me. "Well, Luke doesn't look like he was scraped off the floor of a homeless shelter," he commented, "so my money's on him."

"I think Jace is the Riggs ninja with women," I said, because Jace was standing quiet like he always did. "Swift and silent, but I bet he cleans up."

Jace rolled his eyes and didn't say a damn thing.

"Yeah, the mysterious one," Ryan said, giving Jace his once-over look. "I can see it. So are we going inside to get this done?"

Since we were finished with the who-has-the-biggest-dick conversation (it's definitely me), we trooped into the bank. The manager who'd set the appointment with us was a little surprised to see four degenerates, but this was Detroit, and he looked defeated by life. After we signed a bunch of shit, he led us to a back room with a safe deposit box in it and left us there.

It wasn't a very big box. It was the size of two shoe boxes, just a plain gray metal box sitting on a table. The four of us gathered around it.

"Okay, so it isn't a body," I said. "There's that."

"It could be a hand or an eyeball," Jace pointed out.

"You could fit coke in there," Dex said. "Or heroin."

"Anthrax," Ryan said. "Anthrax isn't very big."

"You know he wanted this, right?" Dex said, looking around at us with suspicious eyes. "This whole little show was planned before he went inside. He wanted us all to gather here, stare at this box, just like we're doing now. We're doing exactly what he wanted."

I ran a hand through my hair. None of us trusted Dad as far as we could throw him. I didn't know what was in this box, but whatever it was, it wasn't good.

"Open it," I said to Dex, who had the key in his hand.

"This fucking sucks," he complained again, but he put the key in the box's lock and turned it. He opened the lid and we all peered in.

The box contained four envelopes, one with each of our names on it. They were thick.

I pulled mine out and opened the flap. "Jesus Christ," I said softly.

It was money. Stacks of hundreds, wrapped and compact. Thousands and thousands of dollars—forty, fifty thousand maybe. And that was just my envelope. My brothers had all opened theirs and found the same.

We all locked eyes for a second in shocked silence. Dad didn't have money; he'd never had money. He drove a shitty old pickup truck and our house was falling down. *He suddenly had money to throw around*, Ryan had said to me on the phone.

"Look," Jace said, breaking the silence. "In the bottom."

In the bottom of the box, beneath where the envelopes had been stacked, was a handwritten note.

Just the beginning. Next delivery to the second safe on the 19th. The combination is in the first safe. Don't fuck it up, boys.

"The second safe?" I said.

"Luke," Dex said. I looked up to see his crazy laser gaze fixed on me. "Is there a second fucking safe?"

"No," I said. "I have no idea what he's talking about." There was a safe in the Riggs Auto office with no money in it—I'd looked.

"Think harder," Dex said.

Then it clicked. There was another safe behind the main garage, behind the fence where we kept the cars, splattered with paint and piled behind skids and boxes. I'd assumed it was broken, waiting to go to the junk yard.

"Yeah," I said. "There's a second safe. I've never opened it. I assumed it was garbage."

Dex got a dark look, crazy and calculating at the same time, and for a second I thought he knew a hell of a lot more about this than I did. It was hard to tell with Dex, because he always looked crazy, but I caught his eyes and he looked away.

It was Jace who broke the silence. "I'm not taking this money," he said. "Wherever this came from, it isn't legal." He dropped his envelope back in the box. "I just got out, and there's is no way I'm going back in. Not for any money. Not for anything."

"I'll take mine," Ryan said, putting it in the pocket of his jacket. "I have a kid to raise."

"They could be marked bills," Jace said.

Dex snorted. "That would take some kind of big-league sting operation. No one is going to that kind of trouble for Dad." He put his envelope in his pocket. "I don't know where this came from, and it's probably morally wrong, but I don't give a fuck. I'll take it."

I was quiet, looking at the envelope in my hand. Fifty grand, maybe more.

Don't fuck it up, boys.

"Luke?" Dex said. He was looking at me, his eyes dancing. He was enjoying this. "Are you in or are you out?"

Dad got into some bad shit in the last few years.

When it got hard, you just packed your bags and kept going.

Don't fuck it up, boys.

My throat was thick. I put my envelope back in the box.

"I want to know where this came from," I said. "I mean, I want to know *exactly* where this came from."

"Probably wise," Ryan said.

"Yeah," Dex agreed. "I want to know, too. I'll take a look into it while I spend my money."

"You want to know where it came from," Jace said in his low voice, "there's only one guy to ask."

We looked at each other. Ryan groaned. Dex scrubbed a hand over his face.

"Fuck," he said. "One of us is going to have to see Dad."

EIGHT

Emily

THERE WERE several contenders in the running for the worst day of my life. One of them was prom night, when I spent six hours in the company of Justin Schachter, fighting off his clammy grabby hands and pretending to enjoy myself and actually care about who was prom queen. Another was the last day of my last internship, when they told me I wasn't nice enough to get the job. Apparently I should have smiled more. I'd bitten the insides of my cheeks until they bled, but I'd walked out of there without saying a thing. That was a bad day.

It looked like this day might beat both of them.

I woke up in my old bedroom, in my single bed. Mom was still home when I went downstairs, which was strange, because she usually left for work early, as did Dad. I didn't have to be at Lauren's salon until ten, and she picked me up at nine, so for the few days I'd been home, I'd had the place to myself in the morning.

But Mom was sitting at the kitchen table, fully dressed in her nice work pants and blouse, a cup of coffee in front of her. Like she was waiting for me.

My gut turned. There was something off about Mom and Dad since I'd been home—something off about everyone and everything. There was a strange tension in the air, and Mom kept hugging me and stroking my hair like I was five. Dad didn't say much at all, keeping to his books and newspapers in the living room. He left for work early and worked late. There had been no family dinners since that first night, because we were all so busy —the salon didn't close until seven, and there was cleanup to do after that. I was still learning Lauren's business, and I was putting in the long hours until I had it mastered so she could take some time off.

I stopped in the kitchen doorway and looked at Mom, the unhappy look on her face despite how nice and tidy she was for work. "What is it?" I said.

"Have a cup of coffee, sweetie," Mom said.

But I did not want a cup of coffee. My stomach had just dropped to the floor. "Mom. What is it?" I said again.

"We need to talk."

I took a breath as every possible bad thing came to me, every-thing at once. "Oh, my god. How terrible is it? Do you have cancer?"

"What?" Mom said. "No."

"Does Dad have cancer?" He'd been so quiet, withdrawn, maybe—

"No one has cancer," Mom said firmly.

"Then tell me. Just tell me."

She sighed and shook her head. "You never did take bad news well. You overreact."

And now she'd just admitted it was bad news. "Mom!"

"All right. Lower your voice." She winced. "You may have

noticed that your father is a little distant since you've been home. There is a reason for that."

I sank into a kitchen chair, my knees suddenly weak.

"The fact is," Mom continued, "your father and I are having some difficulties. And we're taking some time apart."

For a second, I was too stunned to speak. People's parents split up all the time—most of my friends' parents were split—but *my* parents? Mom and Dad? They were a unit, indivisible. Our family was functional, happy. Mom and Dad raised us as a team, everyone knew that.

I mean, they weren't very romantic. They didn't hold hands or go on dates or anything like that. But whose parents were romantic? Did that matter? Was it supposed to matter? Should I have seen?

Then the penny dropped.

First: Lauren wasn't here for this conversation. Which meant *Lauren already knew*.

And second: "Wait a minute," I said. "You're taking a break? As in it's already happening? But you're both here."

Mom sighed and looked at me meaningfully, and I knew. I hadn't seen Dad in the mornings. And he'd been around after work, but I'd never seen him get ready for bed.

I couldn't help it; my voice rose, making Mom wince again. "Dad doesn't *live* here?"

Mom's voice stayed calm and level. "Your father moved into his own apartment four weeks ago."

"Four *weeks?*" I sounded shrill and crazy, and I couldn't help it, and I didn't care. "You two split up four weeks ago and didn't tell me? And then you pretended that Dad lives here for the past three days?"

"We were going to tell you," Mom said, picking up her untouched coffee and standing, "but you were at the end of your internship, and you were under stress. And it was a very hard time for your father and me." She walked to the sink and dumped the cup out, a little vigorously.

"So what you're saying is, telling me about it would have made it worse."

"I'm saying that it was very hard, and we made the best decisions we could."

"You told Lauren! And she played along with this little fiction that Dad lives here!"

Now Mom's mouth was pressed into a firm line. "We told Lauren because there were reasons we had to. She's been very supportive, despite her own problems."

"What problems?" God, why did no one tell me anything?

"You'll have to ask her that." Mom crossed her arms. "It's her story to tell. This is a small town, Emily. People talk. Your father and I have been trying to keep our privacy. And frankly, that's our right."

I stared at her. This was my mom—I recognized her, everything about her, from the line of her posture to the braid of her hair. And yet in this minute, parts of her were unfamiliar. Her outfit, I realized, was relatively new, and her shoes were flats with beadwork on them. I'd never seen those shoes before. It bothered me suddenly that I didn't know my mother owned beadwork flats, wore them to work.

"Is that all, then?" I asked her. "Is that all I need to know, or is there more?" A horrifying thought occurred to me, but I tried to keep my voice calm. "Is there someone else in the picture? For either of you?"

"No," my mother said firmly, and I felt a wash of relief. "It's nothing like that, honey, I promise you. We've just been together a long time, and people change. And we've found it harder and harder to be together. But your father is coming to the ceremony tonight, so I ask that you keep our business private. Okay?"

Jesus. That was tonight—Mom's big award ceremony, getting

honors from the police force. That was why she was telling me now—so that I would go to the ceremony and pretend our family wasn't splitting up.

I wanted to shout at her, at Dad, at Lauren. It was childish, but there it was. I'd never been the kind of person to swallow down pain and pretend it wasn't happening; I'd always been the one to blow up, quickly and loudly, and get it out of my system before moving on. People called it drama, but to me it was just *feeling* things, really feeling them all the way down to my bones, and dealing with those feelings while they were part of me. I didn't know any other way to do it.

But I looked at the misery stamped on Mom's face, and this time I swallowed it back. I said, "I won't say anything."

Mom's expression softened. "Oh, sweetie," she said, and it sliced me open, that she knew me so well. "This won't change things. You'll see."

She was lying, but I was twenty-six, not five. I'd just have to deal.

But I hated it. I fucking hated it. That, I already knew.

"THANK GOD SHE FINALLY TOLD YOU," Lauren said. We were in her hair salon, The Big Do, sitting in the office at the back while the customers got their hair and nails done in the front. Lauren was sitting in the room's spare chair, wearing yoga pants and an oversized T-shirt with flip-flops. "It was getting really weird in that house."

"They pretended Dad lived there," I said. "For three days. I repeat: *they pretended Dad lived there for three days.* And you went along with it. Come on—doesn't that mean our family is crazy? Or at least definitely weird."

"It was the easiest," Lauren said, shrugging. She had tied her hair back loosely, and strands fell along the graceful line of her neck. I'd never had any problem getting guys to notice me, but secretly I'd always been jealous of Lauren's elegant looks. "No one wanted to just jump you with it when you walked in the door."

"A phone call would have worked," I said. I was sitting behind the desk, where Lauren usually sat. The computer was on in front of me, and we were supposed to be going through the bookkeeping system so I'd know how to make the entries. I lifted my hand, my thumb and pinky in the universal mime-sign for telephone. "Hello, Emily, your father has moved out. Thanks, bye."

"You would have freaked," Lauren said. "You would have dropped everything and come running or something. You would have called Dad crying and yelled at him."

I frowned. The thing was, I sort of would have done that. Mom was smart to tell me while Dad was at work, because freakout or not, I would never call him at the office to dump personal shit on him. I would just wait until he got home, then dump it in a giant tsunami.

But he wasn't coming home.

"Wait," I said. "I don't even know where Dad lives. Where does Dad *live?*"

"He got an apartment on Wilmot Street," Lauren said. "It's sort of cute, but it's also sort of sad. He's got a reading chair and a table and a bed and not much else. I went over there and he had two boxes of Jell-O in his cupboard. What does Dad think he's going to do with Jell-O?"

I ran my hand through my hair. "Fuck my life."

"I think he just reads there, like he always did in the living room," Lauren said. "It's a transplant of the living room. He hasn't talked to me about it much, except to say that everything will be all right."

That sounded like Dad. I put my head in my hands, my elbows on the desk, and groaned.

"See?" Lauren pointed out. "Drama."

"There's nothing wrong with drama," I said. "And by the way, Mom told me you have some kind of problem you're not telling me about. Care to clear the air?"

Lauren's mouth snapped shut, and she swallowed.

"Spill it," I said, lifting my head and glaring at her. "It's time for the drama, Lauren. You can't put it off anymore. *Spill.*"

The muscle in her jaw twitched. "Vic and I are getting a divorce," my sister said.

I stared at her, shocked.

"I can't have kids." The words seemed to be spilling out of her, like I'd pushed a button on a vending machine. "We tried everything, including IVF. It took most of our money and we're broke, and our marriage isn't working anymore. We do nothing but fight. He wants kids." She blinked hard, fighting back tears. "I wanted kids too, but now I'm kind of relieved because it's over. And that makes me a terrible person. So yeah, that's the problem. That's what's going on."

I felt like someone had punched me in the stomach. Mom's news had been shocking, but this... this hurt. This was Lauren, my twin, my other half, and she was in awful pain. Her pain was my pain—it always had been.

I was sick over it. I was sorry for her. I was guilty, because I'd left town and stayed away for eight years. But Jesus Christ, had no one in my family ever learned to use a telephone?

"Don't yell," Lauren said, reading my face. "Don't."

Right. Even when they were telling me their lives were wrecked, apparently no one wanted me to yell. "This is why you need me here?" I said, calmly. "This is why you need my help to run the shop?"

"I need a break." Her voice cracked a little on the last word, like she was fighting tears. "I work long days, seven days a week. We have to sort through our things and sell the house and see the lawyers... the real estate agent... the bank..." She closed her eyes and rubbed her forehead. "Please don't yell at me, Em. I just need some help, okay?"

I stood up, came around the desk, and pulled her out of her chair. I wrapped my arms around her for the first time in years and gave her a bear hug, tight to me. She didn't respond at first, then lightly patted my back in her dignified way.

"Thanks," she said.

"I'm going to kill him," I said.

"Don't."

"I will," I insisted. "I will murder his worthless fucking hide. I'll do it. He is fucking dead."

She sighed against me, but the sound was sort of amused. "You don't have to kill anyone, Em," she said.

"I so do," I said. "Now let's finish up, so you can get out of here."

NINE

Emily

I LASTED until four o'clock before I texted Luke. His number was just sitting there on my phone, with that one word, *Hi*. He wasn't inviting a conversation, not really. And we had nothing to talk about, because my car wasn't fixed yet. Except...

I needed someone to talk to. Anyone, really. Lauren left and I sat out front at the shop's reception desk, answering the phone and cashing people out while the stylists worked. It wasn't hard— I've worked plenty of retail in my life—but I had to act pleasant and normal, like I didn't feel like shouting. And it wasn't working.

Luke and I had never had the kind of relationship where we had long heart-to-hearts, but he knew me. Everything about me. He'd gone to school with me, even during my short-hair phase— ugh—and he knew my family. Maybe we were nothing now, but he'd seen me naked and he'd taken my virginity, and to me that was some kind of a connection. I'd made him mad, but he'd insisted on fixing my car. We were friends—the kind without benefits anymore. So during a lull at the front desk, while I gritted my teeth listening to the stylists chatter behind me, I pulled out my phone and texted him: *I am having the worst day ever. EVER.*

It only took seconds for a reply to pop up. *Again?*

You asshole, I shot back. *I am serious. My parents are splitting, and so are Lauren and Vic.*

There was a pause, obviously of surprise. *That sucks, Em. I'm sorry.*

No one wanted to tell me, I ranted, thumbs flying now. *They all kept it secret. Like they don't trust me. Mom says I overreact.*

Well...

Shut up. Do your brothers keep secrets from you?

Em, Luke wrote, *I don't even know where Dex lives. I'm serious.*

Okay, so the Riggs family was maybe more dysfunctional than mine. I'd give him that. Though I hadn't known where my dad lived until a few hours ago. It still stung.

As for my father, Luke texted, *yeah, I'd say he has some fucking secrets.*

Now this was good. *What does that mean?*

Just that he's an asshole, Luke wrote, *and now he's an asshole whose problems are mine.*

I stared at the words. I wondered what his father had done—besides get drunk and try to run someone over, that is.

Yeah, Luke's family was definitely worse than mine.

A customer came through the door, and I had to put my phone down. Then the salon phone rang. I dealt with one thing after another and an hour later I picked my phone up again and saw that Luke hadn't sent anything else. I felt a shot of disappointment, because I wasn't done talking to him. It looked like I would have to start the conversation again. Which made me think of a question.

So I texted him: *Who started it?*

It took him a minute to answer. *Who started what?*

Us, I wrote. *Me and you. Eight years ago. I remember making out the night of the big football game, but I don't remember who started it.*

I smiled to myself. That was a good memory, and I hadn't let myself think about it in a long time. Westlake High's football team had made it to the league championship finals, and everyone, literally *everyone,* had gone to the game—except me and, apparently, Luke Riggs. I'd stayed away out of spite, because I'd dated the quarterback and he'd just dumped me because I wouldn't put out. Luke had stayed away because he was a badass who didn't give a shit. I'd run into Luke at the Fire Pit, the spot where everyone usually hung out, which was deserted that night. He was wearing low-slung jeans and a worn dark green jacket, scruff on his jaw. And somehow we'd ended up at Shaunnesy Beach in the dark and the cold, making out in his dirty old truck.

And it was the best thing *ever.* I could still remember the feel of his hands on my skin that night, how they were warm and strong and I wanted them everywhere. I could still remember how my entire body hummed. I'd dated guys, and I'd made out with them, but I'd never had sex, and that night I knew why. Because none of those guys had made me feel like *that.*

My phone buzzed with a text. *You started it,* Luke wrote.

I don't remember that, I wrote back.

His reply was immediate. *Definitely you.*

Did I jump him? I didn't usually jump guys, but then again, this was Luke. *But you drove me to Shaunnesy Beach in your truck,* I argued. *Did I tell you to do that?*

You told me you wanted to go somewhere, anywhere, Luke wrote back. *You think I was gonna fucking say no?*

No, Luke wasn't the type to turn me down when I suggested something. But he had let me do the suggesting, instead of pushing me in to things. It was one of the things that had made me trust him despite his bad reputation.

Despite the string of secret makeout sessions that followed that first one, he hadn't even pushed me into sex. That, I remembered. The sex had been my idea, and Luke had happily obliged. And wow, had he ever.

Now, that—*that* was a good night.

You're a gentleman, I teased him. *Driving a girl around when she asks.*

Are you fucking kidding me? Luke wrote back.

I laughed to myself, but the laugh came with a shiver. God, we'd had amazing sex. Amazing. And it had been fun. Since Luke, sex hadn't been fun. It had been more like a drive toward a goal—for both the man and me. To get laid, to get a boyfriend, a girlfriend, a date to show off, a relationship, even just an orgasm. There was always an equation: *What am I getting out of this? What is he getting? Am I getting enough? Is he getting enough? Is someone going to want more?* It was exhausting, and eventually I'd just given up and sworn off men, because why have sex at all when there was no fun in it? I could just have an orgasm on my own.

But I couldn't have a Luke Riggs orgasm on my own. No, I could admit that. The problem was that Luke himself was right on the other end of my phone, and he wasn't mad at me anymore. And he was still badass. And suddenly I wondered what would happen if I asked. If I started it again.

Probably a bad idea.

THREE HOURS later I was sitting in the stuffy auditorium of a banquet hall, watching my mother get her award. I had Dad sitting on one side of me and Lauren on the other. We'd already done pre-ceremony drinks and appetizers in which we'd all stood awkwardly, trying to pretend things were normal. Mom and Dad always had three feet between them, like they were magnets pointing the wrong way. Lauren didn't have Vic with her—she told everyone he had to work late. Dad only patted my arm when I saw him and said, "Please don't make a fuss, Em. Please. Everything is going to be okay."

If one more person told me not to make a fuss, I thought I might scream.

My jaw hurt. I was wearing a navy blue sundress with small white dots on it, paired with a white cardigan over my shoulders. I'd put my hair down and curled it, added understated makeup and silver hoop earrings. The people who came by—Mom's coworkers, other officers and their families, the chief of police, a few other big Westlake dignitaries—looked at me with polite surprise. *Why, you're Lauren's sister! The other daughter! We thought you'd left town!* I'd explained twenty times that I was back now, helping out at Lauren's salon. There were a lot of covert glances at my left hand. One woman, who worked as a file clerk at the police station, told Lauren and me, "You have to give her grandkids. She's waiting!"

I stiffened, thinking about Lauren, but she reached behind me and pinched my ass, making me jump. "Let it roll off, sis," she whispered.

I could do that. I could sit in the dark and watch the boring speeches until Mom was called to the podium. I could stand and clap with the rest of the room, giving her a standing ovation. She was my mom. I could do that.

But the minute it was finished, I snuck off to the hallway by the ladies' room and pulled out my phone.

Where are you right now? I texted Luke.

This time it took him a few minutes to reply, long enough for me to start to panic. Maybe he was bored of me, or still mad.

Maybe he was out with someone else. Maybe he had someone and hadn't mentioned it? Who the hell was Luke seeing? I mean really, who was she? Was she pretty? I had to know.

Sorry, he wrote, the text popping up while I sweated. *I was out behind the garage.*

It was late, and the body shop was closed. *What were you doing there?* I asked.

It doesn't matter, he replied. *Where are you?*

Mom just got her award, I told him.

Okay then, Luke wrote. *That's nice.*

The Riggs brothers had no reason to love the Westlake PD, so for some reason Luke was being pleasant. Polite, even. So I texted: *Are you trying to get laid?*

Well, shit, he wrote, and I could hear his slow, sexy drawl in the words. *I am now. You offering?*

That was a good question. The million-dollar question, really. I knew it was a bad idea to start this, and yet I was doing it. Why?

He was hot—that was one thing. Good God, was he hot. College didn't produce any specimens like Luke Riggs, and the corporate world afterward sure as hell hadn't either. Any girl would think Luke was sexy, but his particular hotness drove me a little crazy. I went out of my mind. I became a girl who would jump a guy she wasn't supposed to in his truck and offer up her virginity. A girl who would sneak into his room after that, with no one knowing, to get as much of him as she could.

I hadn't been that girl in eight years. I hadn't *thought* about that girl in eight years, and I realized now that had been on purpose. I had pushed her away, silenced her, pretended she'd never existed.

I looked around the banquet hall, at my family and the people of Westlake. To them, I was one version of Emily Parker. Everyone saw Emily Parker, cop's daughter and all-around decent—if a tad dramatic—young woman. Someone who should settle down and get to producing grandkids. College and work had seen Emily Parker the go-to achiever who couldn't quite get as far as she wanted and eventually gave up. Probably to go home and start making grandkids.

But Luke Riggs was the only one who saw wild Emily. The girl who broke the rules and wasn't cautious. The girl who pursued pleasure because she liked it, and she didn't apologize for it because Luke never expected her to. That girl had been exciting and fun, and I didn't want to silence her anymore. I wanted to be her, even if it was just for a few hours.

I knew what eighteen-year-old Emily would do in this situation, so I texted Luke: *Fine, I'm offering.* Then grown-up Emily added: *I'm so weak.*

Seven months without dick, Em, Luke wrote. *You should know better.*

He knew me so well.

You're right, I'm not thinking straight, I wrote. *Help me make a good decision here.*

His reply was: *Get over here and take your clothes off.*

My body decided for me, with an all-over shiver that went straight down my spine and tingled up between my legs. Cold sweat started on my lower back, and I tugged the white cardigan tighter around myself to hide my hard nipples.

I walked calmly across the room and found Lauren. Mom and Dad were in the middle of a knot of people congratulating them, so I said to Lauren, "I'm taking off. Tell Mom and Dad, okay?"

She looked at me with her terrifying twin sister X-Ray vision. "You don't have a car," she said, like she was Sherlock Holmes and she was pointing out a clue.

"There are cabs in Westlake," I said. "At least there used to be. I'm going to take one."

"Really?" The X-ray turned up a notch. "Where are you going?"

"Going out for a drink with a girlfriend. That's why it's best I don't drive."

"What girlfriend?"

Damn, she knew all the same people I did. "Tracy Harding," I said in a flash of inspiration. Tracy and I had hung out a few times in high school, and Lauren loathed Tracy—something to do with Tracy coming on to Vic at a party.

Sure enough, Lauren looked like she smelled something awful. "Tracy Harding is your girlfriend?"

I shrugged. "I've been in town four days. Beggars can't be choosers. See you tomorrow."

She narrowed her eyes and stared at me harder. "You're lying about something, but I don't know what, and I don't have time to get it out of you right now."

That was rich, coming from the woman who had participated in the Great Dad Deception, but I shrugged. I was going to get laid, incredibly, by the hottest guy in Westlake, and nothing could touch my bubble. "See ya," I said, and left her there, staring after me.

It was a warm June night, and as I waited for the cab I pulled off my cardigan. The summer wind blew my hair, cooled the heat in my neck and my cheeks. I was going to the wrong side of the tracks, and I didn't feel a damn bit sorry.

TEN

Emily

I HAD the taxi let me out at a strip mall a few blocks from Luke's place. When your mother is Westlake's most prominent police officer, someone is eventually going to talk. At eighteen I'd had my own car, and I'd usually parked it here, in front of the vacuum store that never seemed to do any business and that Luke and I always joked was probably a mafia front. At least no one ever saw me parked in front of the Riggs place, which would have been a disaster.

Nothing much had changed, I noticed as I walked down the street to the house. The Riggs property was pretty big, planted with mature trees, the neighbors hundreds of feet away. There were still weeds everywhere, the walkway was cracked, and some of the boards of the front porch were rotted. I could see the guest house behind the main building, where Luke and I had spent all of our time. It was dark and missing a few shingles, but otherwise it looked just as it did eight years ago.

The house was dark, too, except for one light on the main floor. I'd only been in the house once or twice, when Luke brought me there when no one else was home. It had been fun, sneaking in sex on the living room couch, but I hadn't had any desire to have one of Luke's brothers walk in, so we'd kept to the guest house as a rule.

Rules, I thought as I walked up the wooden porch steps in the dark. *I need to set some rules.* We weren't teenagers anymore, overrun with hormones. I needed to make it clear that this was just sex, nothing else. That it might be tonight only. That we were going to be careful that no one could know. That I wasn't staying the night. Yes, that was definitely a good idea. I would—

I raised my hand to knock, but the front door opened before I could do it, revealing a dark shadow in the doorway. A dark, looming shadow that was utterly familiar and smelled like laundry soap and male skin and sweaty sex.

He took my arm and pulled me through the doorway, his touch slow and warm. He closed the front door behind me and backed me against it, caging me in with his big, stupidly hot arms. And Luke Riggs leaned close, his breath against my neck, and nipped me gently at the curve of my jaw.

I opened my mouth to say something, but all that came out was a moan.

Luke touched his tongue to the spot he'd just bitten, soothing it, and Jesus, I was already wet between my legs. I'd had sex— actual sex—with guys who didn't make me as hot as Luke did with one lick of his tongue. I placed my palms flat against the door behind me and tried to hold myself up. "Luke," I managed.

"I told you to take your clothes off," he said in a rough voice in my ear, and I went hot all over. Just like that, we were playing a game. One we'd played before, that we both knew and liked. The rules were this: Luke took charge and got bossy, but he was still mine to control. He used his voice and his touch and his tongue, and he said dirty things to me, but I could always get away from him, or push him, or say no.

I loved this game. I never, ever said no.

"I know," I said to him, my voice a breath.

He placed a fingertip deep in the vee of my neckline, between my breasts. Then he drew it up slowly, over my breast-bone and my clavicle and up the line of my neck, his mouth still close to the skin beneath my ear, his other arm still caging me. I felt my pulse pounding in my throat beneath his touch.

"Seven months, Em," he said in his sexy rasp. "You need to be fucked properly. By me. Now take this dress off before I rip it off you."

I didn't need any other prompting. I pulled down the side zipper and shrugged the dress off my shoulders, letting it drop to the ground. I stepped out of it and kicked it away.

Luke tutted, moving his fingertip beneath the strap of my bra. "Now this."

I unclasped the bra and dropped it. I kicked off my mule sandals, too, so now I was just in my panties, white lace against my skin.

He straightened the arm that was caging me and looked down at me, even in the almost-dark, taking his time. "Still that smoking hot body," he commented, giving me a little thrill. I didn't look like I had at eighteen, but I hoped I looked pretty good. He drew his finger down around the curve of my breast, traced it over my hard nipple. Moved his hand down my stomach, lower.

"Do you..." I tried to speak while my brain shouted *lower, lower, keep going, lower.*

His hand paused below my belly button. "Do I what?"

I was playing the game. "Do you... want my panties off?"

"Hmm," Luke said, a pure male sound deep in his throat. His hand moved lower again, moving under the waistband of my panties, and my legs parted as he slid his fingers down between them. He leaned his mouth to my ear again. "Do you think I want your panties off?"

I couldn't think. No words were forming, in either my head or my mouth. Just a pure signal of pleasure as his fingers moved into my pussy and started to rub. His big, rough, work-hardened fingers on my tender flesh, his thumb brushing gently over my clit. My head thumped back against the door as I gasped for breath, over and over.

Then I couldn't breathe, because he put his mouth on mine and kissed me. A long, slow, deep kiss, possessive and a little hard. He licked his tongue into my mouth and it felt so good, so familiar and new at the same time, that I gave in completely. I let him suck my tongue and rub my pussy and pin me to the door. Then he broke the kiss, hooked his fingers into the hips of my panties, and got to his knees.

It wasn't possible that something this good was happening to me. I was having a wild erotic dream where Luke Riggs, fully clothed in jeans and a tee, was pulling my panties off and putting his mouth between my legs. The first time he ever did this to me we were eighteen, in the back of his truck, and it was so good I just about screamed. This time promised to be better.

I could feel his scruff against the insides of my thighs. I could feel his hands pulling my legs apart. Then I could feel his mouth, his tongue traveling my throbbing skin, rubbing and exploring in an open-mouthed kiss. My knees shook and I pressed myself into the door to stay upright. I tilted my head back and I pushed my hips forward into his face, and he took me greedily, using his mouth, sucking on me, making me wetter than I already was. God, his mouth was pure sin, and I hadn't felt anything like it in eight years. I whimpered against the door as he moved just so, right over my clit, and gave it slow, hot attention, like it was the best thing he'd ever tasted. He sucked it softly and swiped his tongue around it, then over it, then again.

I went off like a rocket, shouting and writhing, the pleasure hitting me so hard it was almost painful. I didn't hold back; I just let it take me, and I let go. It was fucking incredible, and when I came to, panting, he was holding me up so I wouldn't fall to the floor.

Luke stood up, wiped his arm over his mouth—why that was so goddamned hot, I had no idea, but it made me weak—and took my hand without a word. Then he led me upstairs.

It was dark up here, but he knew where he was going. He led me, buck naked, to a bedroom and pulled me inside. I sat on the bed, and he pulled his shirt off over his head, and oh, I was ready again.

It was almost dark, but I could see his muscled body, the tat on his arm, the dark dusting of hair on his chest and stomach leading down into his jeans. He looked different than he had eight years ago, thicker and more heavily muscled, but he was the same gorgeous work of art. He unbuckled his belt and pushed his jeans and boxer briefs down in one motion while I watched the show. His thighs were strong and dusted with the same dark hair, his hips were lean, his stomach flat and rippled, and when he kicked his clothes off and stood straight again his cock stood out thick and hard. For me.

I knew every inch of him. I scooted back on the bed, lying crosswise, and leaned back on my elbows, slowly raising my eyes up to his.

Luke stepped forward to the edge of the bed, looking down at me. He casually put a hand on my bent knee and pushed it aside so my legs were open. This was still the game, but not the game, because he said, "Tell me what you want."

I watched him, standing there between my legs, his cock out and ready. I wanted that. I wanted everything in my life to be blank except that. "Fuck me hard," I told him.

He looked down, his dark lashes against his cheeks, looking

down at my open legs. He brushed my other knee aside so he had a better view, and he took it in, his gaze black. "You look as good as I remember," he said roughly.

You look better than I remember, I wanted to say, but the compliment felt too raw. Instead I leaned back, letting him have a good view, and I teased him. "I'm not as good. I'm better."

"Don't make promises you can't keep."

I lowered a hand between my legs, where he was looking, and crooked a finger at him. "Come here, Mr. Big, and find out."

"Fucking hell," he said. He leaned to the nightstand and pulled open the drawer, taking out a box of condoms.

"Brand new box?" I said, seeing that it was unopened. *Good,* the bitch part of me gloated. *He isn't mid-box.*

Luke opened the box and looked at me from under his lashes. "I bought them when you sent that first text," he said. "I know when you want to fuck, Em. Usually before you do."

I couldn't argue with that, and besides, he'd opened a condom and was rolling it on. Another thing that shouldn't be hot but made my insides clench, I wanted him so bad. I watched him in a lust-filled stupor.

"Ready?" he said when he was finished. He leaned forward and put one knee on the bed. "You better be."

I pulled him down to me and kissed him, deep. He braced himself over me, broke the kiss, and pushed into me, running his teeth lightly over my lower lip. I moaned. It felt so *good.* But he was taking his time, pushing me open, pushing all the way in, and I wanted oblivion.

"More," I begged him.

He put one hand on my thigh and pulled out, slamming into me. He still had one foot braced on the floor, and his heavy weight made it hard, just like I wanted it.

"More," I said again.

Luke did it again, and again, until he was in a rhythm. It was deep with an edge of rough, his fingers digging into my thigh and his hips slamming into mine, and my mind became a blank white slate of pleasure. I let everything go: my niggling thoughts, my worries, my regrets. There was just Luke's gorgeous body and his scent that made me high and his hands on me, his cock in me. I had to brace one hand above my head so I wouldn't get slammed into the wall. The other I put on his back, gripping him, feeling his muscles flex over and over as he rode me.

I had no idea what kind of god had made Luke Riggs, but in that moment I was thankful to her. I was downright religious.

His hand let go of my thigh and moved between my legs, and I felt myself losing it again. "Luke—"

"You're coming with me," he said.

"God, it's—"

"Do it."

Another climax rolled through me, and my hips lifted off the bed. Luke pushed me down again, pushed deep, and came, making a sound in his throat that was deep, utterly masculine, and kind of sweet, like he had been pent up for a while. Like me.

We caught our breath like that for a minute, Luke's hands on the bed where his arms were braced, my hand still over my head, the other still on his back. He lowered his head for a second. Then he pulled out of me and stood, turning and walking to the bathroom.

I watched through an orgasmic haze as his amazing ass walked away. And when it disappeared through the doorway, I summoned my voice and said, "Luke."

"Yeah?" he said from the bathroom. He hadn't even bothered to turn on the light.

"I hope you don't think we're finished, because we're not."

ELEVEN

Luke

I MADE A SMALL CHOKING SOUND, not quite a laugh. I finished up and walked back into the bedroom, where Emily was still sprawled on the bed where I'd left her. She looked like she couldn't move.

She watched me walk toward her without even trying to hide it. She'd seen me naked plenty of times, but she still looked kind of fascinated. I took that as a good sign.

I lifted her legs and swiveled her boneless body, then pulled the bedcovers down. "Em," I pointed out, "I just fucked the hell out of you."

"I know," she said in a dreamy voice as she watched me get in bed next to her. "It was a start."

I lay on my back in the dark. I'd just come so hard I saw stars, and it did a lot to relieve the tension after today. Seeing my brothers again, that scene at the bank, the money, the second safe behind the shop that I'd found the combination to and opened—

all of that was going to eat at me. I knew that. But right now I was in bed with Emily, smelling sex, my mind drifting. I couldn't put two thoughts together, which was the way I wanted it, at least for now.

She slid under the covers and rolled on to me, her arm slung over my chest, her face buried in the side of my neck, like we did this all the time. Like we'd just done it last night, and the night before that.

I blinked in the dark, swallowed. I put my arm around her and stroked her shoulder. She pressed even closer to me, warm and smelling of woman, and put her cheek against my skin. It was a bona fide cuddle, and I pressed my advantage, running my hand over her side to her waist while she practically purred.

This was the Emily I remembered. She always changed after I'd made her come a few times—she lost her edge and got soft and sweet. Affectionate, even. Like we were a couple, even though we weren't. But in those hours at night a long time ago, we'd pretended we were.

Now she ran her fingers through the hair on my chest and my stomach, then leaned up on one elbow and kissed my pec. "Do you still hate having your nipples touched?" she asked.

"Don't go there," was my answer. I hated that.

I felt her smile against my skin. She kissed me lower and ran her hands over me appreciatively, which wasn't the worst thing in the world, so I just lay there and let her do it. I watched her blonde hair trickle over my skin as she kissed lower, and I found myself reaching out and running my fingers through the strands, watching its pretty gold against my hands. She was a natural blonde, and I could never get all of the grease off my fingers since I'd started back at the body shop. Part of me was still surprised Emily let me touch her at all.

She kissed my stomach, then sighed in her dreamy way. "You

didn't gain any weight," she said. "Trevor Halbersen gained weight. He looks like someone stuffed a pillow down his shirt."

That was good, because Halbersen was the football jock who had dumped Emily in high school for not putting out. "You fuck him too?" I asked, the words coming out harsher than I intended as I watched my fingers touch her hair.

"No," Emily said. "I ran into him in the Price Mart. He looks like a fifty-year-old PTA dad, and you have these." She pressed her fingertips into my abs, which I flexed for her obligingly.

"You picked the right guy, then," I said.

"Duh," she replied. She was always a little goofy when she was drunk on sex. Which was why I'd tried to keep her drunk on sex. It was always the moment with us—just the moment. Just the two of us doing what we wanted together for a little while. She explored my abs for another minute, like she hadn't seen any in a long time, then moved down, down.

I grunted as she stroked her fingers up my dick, which was still recovering. "Emily, I'm not eighteen anymore."

"Be quiet," she said in her sex-drunk voice. "Your cock and I haven't seen each other in eight years, and I'm saying hello."

I didn't know whether to laugh or wince, because she leaned down and brushed her lips over it while it was still oversensitized. I realized she'd actually given it a kiss, a rather sweet one, like she was glad to see it. I lifted my eyes to the ceiling and took a breath, because having Emily Parker kiss your cock is, once again, not the worst fucking thing in the world. Also, she was making it wake up again.

"I knew it," I said as she kissed her way back up my stomach again.

"Knew what?"

"You haven't been properly laid in eight years."

That made her look up at me, pushing her hair back from her eyes. "I've been laid plenty, thank you," she said.

"Not true," I said. "And whatever you got was crappy. I can tell."

"I have had very fulfilling sex."

"Then why did you swear off men?"

Her lips pressed together in a line. "Well, you attacked me like a starving man attacks a steak. I don't think you've had a nonstop porn party, either."

"I was never in one place very long," I said. "No relationships. I never saw anyone more than once."

I didn't know why I told her that. It wasn't the kind of thing I talked about. Emily frowned, still looking at me from above my stomach. "Hmm," she said.

I frowned back at her. "What?"

"I might be an awful person," she confessed, "because I'm kind of happy about that. I hate thinking there was some girl who was prettier and more awesome than me."

I felt a smile tug my mouth. Yeah, she was as humble as ever. "So really it's all about your ego," I pointed out. "Not my happiness."

She sat up and straddled me, letting me see everything in all its full glory—her tits (36C, you think I didn't fucking know?), her slim torso, her hips, her perfect thighs squeezing me, her blonde hair in sex-tousled curls over her shoulders. "Luke," she said, rolling her eyes, "me and my ego *are* your happiness. I mean, come on." She gestured to herself, then did a little wiggle with her hips that sent shock waves straight to my cock. "Aren't you happy right now?"

"No," I said, and in one move I hauled her off me and flipped her onto the bed, facedown. I rolled on top of her and pinned her gently, rubbing my half-hard cock into the crack of her ass. "Now, maybe," I allowed, a growl in her ear. "Now I'm happy."

She was laughing into the pillow, but she slowed and bucked

her hips up off the bed, pressing her ass into me and rubbing. "Oh, god," she said in a half-moan. "Tell me we're doing it again."

I reached down and cupped her ass, then gave it a quick, stinging slap. "Only if you're good." She moaned again, and I said, "We do it my way this time."

She wasn't laughing anymore. "Okay, Luke," she said.

I leaned down and let the scruff on my jaw scrape the tender skin of her neck. "Open your legs," I told her.

She did.

Oh yes, she did.

It was a long night.

And Emily was right.

For the first time in eight years, I was pretty fucking pleased.

TWELVE

Emily

"I'D LOVE to help you, honey," my mother said, "but I don't think that's a good idea."

I sighed and swiveled in my chair, watching through the office doorway as the stylists in the salon swept the floor and gossiped. We had a small lull with no customers, and things were under control. I needed to go pick up my car, which Luke had texted me was now fixed. The problem was, I needed a ride.

"Why isn't it a good idea?" I asked Mom. "You just need to take me to Riggs Auto and drop me off. I'll take it from there."

"It just isn't," Mom said. She added tightly, "You couldn't get your car fixed at any other place in town?"

Right. Mom was a cop, Mike Riggs was in jail, and everyone assumed Luke was a dirtbag just like his father. And no one—least of all my mother—knew that three days later, I was still riding high from the night of orgasms I'd had in Luke's bed. I'd snuck home at four in the morning that night, tiptoeing into my bedroom while Mom was still asleep. God, I still couldn't believe I was twenty-six. One of these days I'd grow a spine.

"Luke isn't so bad," I heard myself say. "I went to high school with him. He's giving me a deal."

"I recall perfectly well that you went to high school with the Riggs boys," Mom said. "I wouldn't take a deal from any of those kids."

"He's not a kid, Mom. And why are we having this conversation? It's already done, and my car is already fixed. If you won't take me to pick it up, I guess I'll call Dad."

Mom snorted. "He won't do it. He always relied on me to take care of details like this."

Right. My family was cracking up. I tried Dad anyway, getting him at the office a few minutes before he left work.

"I can't do it, Emily," he said when I explained. "I just ordered a new sofa and I'm told it's coming in an hour."

"A new sofa?" Lauren had said Dad had a reading chair and a box of Jell-O. "That sounds permanent."

Dad sighed. "I have to have somewhere to sit. Just stop worrying, okay?"

No. I was going to worry, because Dad had bought a sofa. You buy a sofa when you *don't* plan on moving back into your house with your maybe ex-wife. "Mom already said no," I complained before I remembered who I was talking to.

"She did? Why?"

"Because my car is at Riggs Auto, and she said it wasn't a good idea."

"Yes, that's probably true," Dad said, adding to my bafflement. "What else did she say? Anything about me?"

Oh, Jesus. "Dad, I'm not playing this game."

"She hasn't called me in days. Tell her I need my black dress shoes for work. I forgot them because they're in the closet in the spare room."

I sighed and ran a hand through my hair. "Tell her yourself."

"I would if she'd answer the phone when I call. I even tried a text. I don't even know if it went through. Just tell her when you see her, okay? I have to go meet the furniture guys."

I hung up and swiveled on the office chair again. I actually didn't mind working for Lauren's salon. I had the hang of it now, and it wasn't that bad. Every day was different, there were people coming and going, and I got to be the boss and make decisions. Also, going through the books showed me that the place was nice and profitable. Lauren had picked a good location, with lots of car and foot traffic, and she'd spent years building up a good reputation, making sure she hired the best and friendliest stylists, making sure the place was clean and inviting. The result was a hard-core group of regulars who wouldn't go anywhere else and told their friends.

My sister had done a kickass job, and she was making money, but I could see why she was stressed out. Being the boss meant doing the stylists' schedules, handling things when they were sick or late, and juggling a hundred different questions a day. It meant taking complaints from the customers who couldn't be pleased and handling the hard stuff. Just yesterday the credit card system had gone down for three whole hours, most of which I'd spent on hold, trying to get an answer to when it would be back up again.

But I could handle it. I'd gone to college for business, and since then I'd only had internships where no one let me do a damn thing except sit in meetings and look pretty. I wanted to be in the trenches, making a business run, making money. It helped that I *maybe* had a natural talent for bossing people around. It also helped that during the down times, like now, I got to get my hair cut and my nails done. You took your perks where you could get them.

But it was a drag, not having a car. Lauren dropped me off in the mornings and picked me up at night, and now that I was up to speed, I didn't bother her for the hours in between. I let her deal with her shit instead. I wasn't planning to break the rule now—I'd probably call a cab to pick up my car—but the phone rang in my hand with Lauren's number.

"Everything is fine," I told her when I answered the phone. "You're not missing anything. It's all under control."

"If you say so," Lauren said. "Listen, it's five o'clock and I'm going nuts in this house. Vic is supposed to be home any minute. Want to go out for dinner?"

I glanced out into the salon again. We were open until seven. A customer had come in, and Bettie, one of the stylists, had taken her. Shonda, the junior stylist, was prepping to wash the customer's hair. Darlene, the manicurist, was sitting at her station texting on her phone—she had a customer coming in ten minutes. "It looks pretty calm here," I said to Lauren. "We can eat, and I can come back and help close. And my car is fixed, so you can take me to pick it up and you don't have to drive me around anymore."

"I like driving you around," Lauren argued. "It keeps me away from my almost ex-husband."

This was my life now, listening to two ex-couples complain. Christmas was going to be just dandy. "Well, I want my car back. Come get me."

"Say please, beeyotch," Lauren said, which was what we used to call each other when we were fifteen, but she hung up and twenty minutes later we were in her car. "Are we going to Riggs Auto?" she asked.

"Yes," I said, pressing my hands into my lap so I wouldn't double-check my hair and my makeup. I was wearing shorts, a boho top, and leather sandals, because June was in full swing and it was starting to get hot. I really could not care if Luke Riggs thought I looked good, especially under Lauren's eagle eye. "Why did Mom tell me that having her drop me off was a bad idea?" I asked to change the subject.

Lauren shrugged. She was wearing big sunglasses and a wrap dress, and she looked like a Hollywood star had just decided to start driving around Westlake. "Probably because Mom has been investigating Mike Riggs for, like five years," she said.

My spine went cold, then hot. "What?" I said, but my voice cracked so I tried again. "What do you mean?"

She glanced at me. "I keep forgetting how long you were away," she said. "Mike Riggs is involved with organized crime. Mom was trying to nail him for it."

"Organized crime?" My voice went up. "Like the *mafia*?"

"No, not the mafia," Lauren said. "Like stolen cars. Mom doesn't say a lot of details, but she told me that much."

I thought of Luke's father, a big tall guy with brown hair he'd always kept in a man bun. He had some of his sons' looks, but years of drinking, smoking, and pot made him look like a faded older version. I didn't know him very well, but I'd never seen him do anything except sit around Riggs Auto, smoking and shooting the shit with his mechanics. The man didn't say *crime kingpin* to me, but there was no chance Mom was wrong.

I wondered if Luke knew. I wondered if I should tell him or keep my mouth shut.

What if he knew? What if he'd always known, and he'd never told me?

"Mike Riggs is already in jail," I pointed out to Lauren, hoping I was wrong as hell to even think that about Luke.

"It doesn't matter," she said. "The shop is still open, so the investigation is still on. Whatever's going on will probably go on without him, and Mom plans to stamp it out. I'm sure Mike and his buddies are aware the cops are after them. That's why it's not a good idea for Mom to be driving to Riggs Auto and dropping you off."

Yes, that would be weird. It would also be extra weird if Nora Parker's daughter was, say, sleeping with Mike Riggs' son. Ha ha. Wouldn't that be something?

Whatever's going on will probably go on without him. That meant Luke taking over. But there was no way Luke was taking over his father's criminal business. Was there?

Was there?

I kept my gaze on the road until Lauren pulled in to the parking lot of Riggs Auto. When I moved to open the door, my fingers ached from how tightly I'd been squeezing them in my lap. *Play it cool, Emily, for God's sake.*

One of the mechanics was having a smoke outside the shop's front door, a tall guy with a beer gut and a scraggly beard. He watched both of us with undisguised greed as we walked by. We stepped inside, blinking as we came out of the sunlight, Lauren taking off her sunglasses. Before I could help it, my gaze found Luke.

He was sitting on a wooden chair placed just outside the front reception, wearing jeans and a navy tee, his inked bicep in full view. He was wearing his ball cap again, the brim pulled down and somehow offsetting his gorgeous cheekbones and the scruff on his jaw. He was leaned back in the chair, one arm slung over the back, one black boot resting against the front of a battered old filing cabinet. He was using the foot to leverage himself as he tilted the chair back, balancing it on its back legs. One of the other mechanics was standing next to him, saying something, and Luke was looking down at his lap, listening, the bill of his cap hiding his eyes.

How anyone looked so good while he was doing something as simple as sitting on a chair, tilting it back and listening, I had no idea—but I ate him up. Basically devoured him with my eyes, from his flexing boot straight up his sexy legs to his flat stomach and those shoulders and arms, the tilt of his chin. It occurred to me that I'd taken him for granted eight years ago, because right now I didn't understand why there wasn't a flock of eager women following him around like baby geese.

His chin tilted up and he looked at us, his gaze on me for a hot second before he righted the chair and stood, ignoring the other mechanic and walking toward us. Like last time, he pulled a rag from his back pocket and wiped his hands with it. "Emily," he said in greeting. "Lauren."

"I hear you fixed my sister's shitty car," Lauren said while I stood there with no words in my mouth. Had I ever been around Luke when Lauren was there? Not that I remembered, unless it was in the halls or in class in high school. That final summer, the summer of Luke, Lauren had been wrapped up in her own relationship with Vic, which had been headed for marriage already. She hadn't paid much attention to me or my love life.

"Yeah," Luke said to my sister. "I fixed it the best I can. At least it runs, and will for a little while."

"Uh huh," Lauren said, narrowing her eyes at him. "How much does she owe you?"

He lifted his ball cap, scratched a thumb over his forehead, then put it on again. "We already worked that out," he told her smoothly, his brow rumpled like he was confused she was asking the question. "There's a payment plan."

Lauren looked at me, and I nodded.

"Follow me," Luke said, and turned toward the big garage doors in the back.

We followed, me greedily watching Luke's ass, then cutting my gaze to Lauren to see if she was doing the same thing. She'd never expressed any interest in him, but she was getting divorced now, and come on—hot dirty bad boy mechanic. Lauren was separated, not dead. But her face gave nothing away.

At the back wall of the shop, Luke hit a button and one of the bay doors started to rise. And my sister surprised me by asking him, "How are your brothers doing, by the way?"

"All right, I guess," Luke said as we waited for the door to go up. "Jace is out of prison now and at a halfway house. Ryan is in Detroit, too. He has a son."

"I think I heard about that," Lauren said. If either of them noticed I wasn't taking part in this conversation, they didn't let on. "I'm trying to picture Ryan with a kid."

"No one can picture it," Luke agreed. "Least of all him. We weren't big on parenting in my family."

There it was, Luke's dad, the elephant in the room. But Lauren didn't even seem to notice. "What about Dex?" she asked. "How is he?"

Something trickled up my spine, knowledge that ran deep in my psyche. No one, literally no one, would have heard the subtle note in my sister's voice when she asked that question. But I'd shared a uterus with her, and eight years away or not, I knew Lauren like I knew myself. *Holy shit,* I thought, forgetting my own problems for a second. *Lauren and Dex Riggs?*

Luke shrugged, oblivious to my thunderstruck shock. "Dex is still an asshole," he said. "No surprise there." The bay door was open now and he led us through to the back lot, where my car was parked.

I followed them, my brain working feverishly backward, trying to remember if I'd ever seen Lauren even talk to Dex Riggs. I couldn't recall a single time. Lauren had been with her boyfriend, Vic, since they were sixteen, and she'd married him right before her twentieth birthday. She'd really loved Vic, enough to spend years trying to have a baby with him, enough that she'd needed my help when it fell apart. No way had my sister looked at someone else during her marriage.

But I hadn't imagined that. *What about Dex? How is he?* The divorce wasn't the only secret my sister was keeping from me. I'd bet every last penny I'd ever earn on it.

I was pulled out of my thoughts when we reached my car. Luke opened the driver's door, leaned in to the dashboard—a sliver of his lower back showing as he reached—and stood again, handing me my keys. "Here it is," he said to me. "Get the oil changed once in a while."

"I got the oil changed," I lied outrageously. I never had, because when I went to those places they always tried their hardest to upsell me a bunch of repairs I didn't need. It was probably because of my blonde hair, and I'd hated that I didn't know what was really needed and what wasn't.

So, okay, I sometimes avoided things. Important things.

Luke's expression told me he didn't even consider believing me. "Bring it to me for tune-ups," he said. "Don't bring it to that fuckface Carmichael over on Fifth. He'll charge you three times what I do."

"We don't even know what you *are* charging her," my nosy sister interjected.

But I had it under control now. "Don't worry," I said calmly to Lauren, thinking of the crumpled pile of fives and tens I'd given him. "Luke's rates are very reasonable."

Call me psychic, but I knew he was amused, even though he didn't smile. "Like I say, we worked out a deal," he said.

I took my keys and smiled sweetly at him. "Thank you, Luke," I said. "Maybe I'll give you a tip."

"Always appreciated," Luke said, touching the brim of his ball cap. His eyes beneath the brim lit on me for a hot, incandescent second, and I was amazed the air between us didn't go up in flames. Then he looked away again. "You should go," he said. "Probably best if not many people see you here."

What did he think? That I was going to go straight home and

report on the entire encounter to my mother? I started to protest. "I'm not—"

"We'll go," Lauren said, putting a hand on my wrist and squeezing. But the smile she gave Luke was polite and genuine. "Thanks, Luke. Say hi to your brothers for us."

Luke nodded. "Not likely," he said. "See you later."

"OKAY," Lauren said when we were at the Thai restaurant and our dishes were being put on the table in front of us. "You can tell me the truth. Are you giving Luke Riggs sex to fix your car?"

I gaped at her. Even though I'd seen him naked three days ago, I was still shocked at the suggestion. "Excuse me? No, I'm not." I picked up my chopsticks. "Thanks for basically calling me a prostitute, by the way. Love you too, sis."

She shrugged, picking up her own chopsticks. "Em, he just fixed your car for free."

"Like we both told you, we worked something out."

"Something that doesn't include you giving him any money or your credit card when he gives you your car back," she pointed out.

This was why I'd avoided coming back to Westlake for eight years. Eight years of lovely, nosy-family-free privacy. Right now, I missed those lonely years. "I gave him a deposit, not that it's any of your business," I told her, probably futilely. "I am not giving him sex for car repairs."

It wasn't a lie—I'd given him a hundred bucks, I planned on giving him more, and I wasn't giving him sex for car repairs. I was giving him sex one hundred per cent for free. Frankly, I'd be giving him sex if he'd left me on the side of the road that day. And with the look of him burned on my brain right now, I was wondering when I could give it to him again. I'd thought it might be a one-time thing, but I decided not to fool myself. If Luke didn't have a woman, I was going to go there again.

If he didn't have a woman.

Luke better not have a woman.

"Well, he was giving you a look," Lauren said, poking through her pad thai noodles to find a shrimp. "And he sure grew up hot. Good lord."

I dug my own chopsticks into my rice, stabbing it. I hadn't thought about this aspect of Lauren being single. She'd been off the market so long, I forgot that when it came to Lauren versus me, men usually picked Lauren. "The Riggs brothers are all hot," I said. "At least they used to be."

"Yeah, they were," Lauren said, taking the bait. A little smile crossed her lips. "Remember Ryan in that baseball uniform? We used to go watch his games just so we could look at his ass."

Ryan had been pretty spectacular. "Jace had that broody intellectual thing happening," I said. "That tortured bad boy-poet vibe. You just wanted him to recite something dirty."

"I never thought Jace was as bad as the teachers made him out to be," Lauren said. "He just seemed sort of shy, unlike the others. Like he got a bad rap. Luke had that wickedly cool car, remember?"

I remembered. As soon as he'd turned sixteen, Luke had gotten his hands on an old Mustang that he'd fixed up and painted forest green. The engine had been as loud as a freaking Metallica concert, and he'd roared in and out of the school parking lot every day, leaving a cloud of choking smoke. It drove adults nuts. Even at the time, it had been kind of funny.

I couldn't help prodding for my sister's reaction, so I lied: "I always thought Dex was the hottest Riggs brother, though. I mean, if you like the bad boy thing? He had it in spades."

While Ryan was an athlete and Jace was smart and Luke was just outrageously cool, Dex really was a bad boy. He had the slouch down to perfection and his looks were sleepy and danger-ous, like he'd just come from a wild all-night party. No one had any idea how he passed high school, because he was rarely witnessed actually in class. If there was an award for "Most Likely to Snort Drugs Off a Woman's Ass," Dex Riggs would have won the vote. The fact that he became a cop surprised everyone, and the fact that he was later rumored to be dirty surprised no one at all.

Lauren just looked sad, though, as she looked down into her plate. "Dex isn't redeemable," she said. "He never was."

I stared at her for a long minute, but she didn't elaborate. Okay then. Dex Riggs and my sister—there was *something* there. I just didn't know what.

"Why did we do it?" I asked her.

Lauren looked at me. "Why did we do what?"

"Treat the Riggs brothers like dirt. Like trash. Like everyone told us to." I put my chopsticks down, the thought making some-thing uncomfortable rise in my throat. "Why didn't we just talk to them? Treat them like anyone else instead of like the plague? Make friends with them?" I looked at her. "Why didn't we rebel?"

We hadn't. We'd been good girls, Lauren and me. Cop's daughters. Straight A students. I'd never even gotten a haircut my mother disapproved of, let alone something crazy like a tattoo. Lauren and I were girls who would never date guys like Luke or Dex Riggs—but also girls who would never *talk* to guys like Luke or Dex Riggs.

Until one night, during a big football game, I'd run into Luke Riggs at the Fire Pit.

Even then, I hadn't admitted I'd ever touched him. I still didn't.

And suddenly, that really fucking bothered me.

Lauren didn't know about me and Luke, but she knew what I

meant. She still looked sad, and she shook her head. "They didn't want our friendship, Em," she said. "If we'd offered it, they would have laughed."

"We don't know that," I argued.

"Yes, we do." Anger flitted across her expression, and for some reason I knew she was thinking about Dex. "They would have laughed in our faces. We were at the same school as the Riggs boys, but we were on different planets. And it seems like it should be different now, but now it's worse."

She meant Mom investigating Mike. Mike being in jail. Organized crime. Organized freaking crime. In Westlake.

I bit my lip. Maybe it was noble to think that the differences between Luke and me didn't matter anymore, because we weren't in high school. But I was a realist, and the fact was that by sleeping with Luke, I was still crossing a line.

Chances were, he knew *something* about what his father was up to. Or he was taking over the operation entirely.

He was still on the wrong side of the tracks after all this time.

And I still wanted to cross it if it meant seeing him. I just didn't know what the consequences would be.

THIRTEEN

Luke

WE WERE GOING to draw straws to see who had to go see Dad, but in the end we didn't have to. Jace was exempt, because he'd just left a prison and there was no way he was walking into another one, even for a visit. Ryan begged off because of his kid. I was starting to see how Ryan could just use the words *I have no babysitter* to get out of anything he didn't want—or was too lazy —to do.

That left me and Dex. We tried arm wrestling for it, but it ended in a draw. We were going to do a championship round of rock-paper-scissors, but in the end we just decided we'd both go and share the fucking misery.

That was how I ended up on the two hours' drive with Dex in my car, slouched in the passenger seat. He was wearing sunglasses and half his hair was on end. He was hung over, of course, because Dex was usually hung over. My big brother wore a hangover as often as he wore clothes—probably more often.

The last place I wanted to be going was a prison—Dad's prison. I hadn't visited him yet; none of us had, and we wouldn't be now if it wasn't for that stupid money and the note. No, what I really wanted right now was to have my head under Emily Parker's loose flowered top, inhaling the skin of her 36C's. Because now I'd had a refresher on what they looked, smelled, and tasted like.

Instead I was sitting here with my wreck of a brother, who turned the radio down and rubbed a hand through his hair. "I'll say one thing," he said. "This Charger is fucking boss."

"I know," I said. "It only had a thousand miles on it when I got it. It was a steal."

We talked cars for a few minutes—we'd pretty much learned cars along with our ABC's—and then Dex said, "The house still standing or what?"

This was more interest than he, or any of us, had shown in our birthplace in years, so Dex was making an effort. Or maybe he was just bored. With a psycho, you never know. "Still standing," I said. "That's about all I can say. The place needs pretty much everything, from the roof down."

Dex nodded, like he'd expected that. "You look in the second safe at the shop?"

"Yeah, the combination was in the office safe, like the note said. I opened it. Nothing there."

"Until the nineteenth."

"Right."

Dex seemed to grind the rusty gears of his brain for a second. "Do you need the shop alarm code to get to the second safe?"

I'd already thought of this. If someone was dropping money into that safe behind the garage, they were either climbing the fence or coming through the shop. "Yeah. The fence back there is ten feet high, and I didn't see any signs that anyone's been climbing it."

"So whoever does the drop is either an employee or an outsider who has the alarm codes."

I shrugged.

"The money is handy. Even though it's dirty." Dex patted his pockets, looking for something.

"You spent it already?"

"*Spent* is not exactly precise," Dex said. "I lost most of it at poker night." He pulled a joint from his pocket and patted his clothes again, looking for a lighter.

"What the fuck," I said to him. "Don't light that."

"You're driving, not me," Dex said, ignoring me and lighting up.

"Yeah, and if I get pulled over I'm still fucked."

"So don't get pulled over." He cracked the window halfway. "Jesus, you're getting uptight."

I ground my teeth. It wasn't the joint I was uptight about, it was the fact that I could lose my license, or my car—and he knew it. Because a Riggs without a car was like a Riggs without a dick. Still, there was no way to get Dex to put that thing out unless I fought him for it.

This was why I'd stayed away from my brothers for eight years.

"Are you gonna tell me what you know about Dad?" I said, changing the subject and going on the attack. "Because it was obvious as hell the other day that you knew something you weren't telling us."

"I'm not a cop anymore," Dex said, blowing weed smoke out the window.

"Tell me," I said again.

Dex rubbed his fingers on his temple like his head hurt. "You work with Big Jim at the shop, right?"

"Sure." Big Jim was one of Dad's new dirtbag hires. True to his nickname, he was at least six four and built like a linebacker.

"There are stolen cars moving through Riggs Auto," Dex said. "That's a fact. Big Jim helps Dad run it, and Ronny Red was Dad's partner. That's what Jace told me after he got caught."

I felt my head spinning and I tried to focus on the road. "Jace was stealing cars for *Dad?*"

"Of course he was," Dex said, tossing his joint out the window. "Did you think he was stealing cars for himself? You think it was his own idea? You think that's Jace?"

No. I didn't think that. I'd thought it was out of character for Jace, and now I knew why. Shit, I had to start thinking. "I don't get why," I said. "It couldn't have been for Dad's approval. And I thought Jace had a job." If Jace had enough to live on, he wouldn't go for a life of crime. He'd never been greedy. The Jace I knew always just wanted to get by and, mostly, be left alone.

"Fuck knows why," Dex said dismissively, like he couldn't be bothered to figure Jace out. He'd mostly ignored Jace growing up, like the rest of the world did. "But he was one of Dad's guys."

Until he got busted. Jace hadn't seemed angry, or out for revenge. But he had to feel *something*, doing twenty months in jail for something Dad put him up to.

"Were you investigating Dad when you were on the force?" I asked Dex.

"Not me," Dex said. "I worked robbery, but only in Detroit. Dad keeps his operation local to Westlake. Jace only got caught when he jacked a car in Detroit instead of sticking near home."

I tapped my fingers on the wheel. I'd had a hunch what was happening, but hearing it confirmed burned me up. I'd seen a couple of cars I didn't recognize come and go through the shop, but with the complete lack of records I couldn't be sure they weren't from regulars. The fact that stolen cars were being run under my nose by the assholes who worked for me made me very fucking mad. "So what's our play with Dad?" I asked Dex.

"That depends," Dex replied. "Do we want to run a stolen car business? Or don't we?"

Maybe he had to think about it, but I didn't. "No," I said. "That isn't what I signed up for. Jace already went down for this, and I'm not following him. Neither is Ryan."

"Maybe I don't give a fuck," Dex said.

I glanced at him. "You're trying to tell me you don't care about jail time? Because my bet is the Westlake PD are all over this." It was a pretty educated guess. Dad might have some kind of operation, but he wasn't a criminal genius. No way was he running stolen cars through Westlake without Nora Parker getting wind of it.

Which meant that Emily's mother was most likely investigating my father's criminal activities.

Which meant Emily and I were a bad idea.

I had a feeling I was about to find out just how bad we were.

FOURTEEN

Luke

DAD HAD LOST WEIGHT, and he'd grown a beard. He was wearing old jeans and a denim-colored prison shirt, his hair still long and tied back like he'd always worn it. He was led in to sit behind the Plexiglas partition, and he leaned back in his chair as the guard walked away.

"Well, well," he said. "Two of my boys. I finally got your attention."

Jesus, it was weird to see him. I hadn't actually seen my father in eight years. I hadn't missed him—his lazy attitude, his shitty parenting, his random annoyed punches to the head. He'd given us a roof over our heads and the occasional supply of food, like we were stray dogs he'd let in the house once in a while. I'd had to answer the big questions of life on my own—how to be a good person, how to be a good man, how to find what was going to make me happy. I still hadn't figured out most of that shit, but everything I'd learned, I'd learned alone while I was driving around the country, looking for something I couldn't explain.

So I should have felt nothing. Irritation, maybe, and a dose of pity. Instead, when I looked at him the little kid inside me wondered what I could have been if I'd actually had someone in my corner growing up.

I shut that voice up, hard.

"You have our attention," Dex said. He was sitting in the folding chair next to mine, and I could feel the tension radiating off him like a smell. Whatever his don't-give-a-shit attitude, Dex didn't find this a walk in the park either. "You have fifteen minutes. I don't want to spend any longer than that in this shithole."

"I take it you got my note," Dad said. He stared at Dex, ignoring me for the moment. "Dex, the bigshot cop. Guess it didn't work out quite like you thought, did it?"

Dex had always been Dad's favorite punching bag; he'd taken more flack than any of us. Jace and I could fly under the radar, and Ryan's baseball talent made him partly immune, but something about Dex got under Dad's skin. The idea of Dex becoming a cop had made him angry, which was the only reason Dex had gone through with it.

"Cut the shit," Dex said now.

"Did he tell you he couldn't hack it?" Dad turned to me. "Cracked under pressure, our Dex did. He acts tough, but underneath he's all coward. Went dirty, too."

"Shut up," Dex said, his voice deceptively quiet.

I'd heard rumors about how Dex's career had crashed and burned, but since we weren't exactly close I'd never asked him about it. "Dex isn't dirty," I said to Dad.

Dad just laughed.

"Fuck, why am I even here?" Dex muttered under his breath.

"And you," Dad said to me. He seemed to have been saving

up his hostility, sitting alone in a cell. "Thought you could just walk away, like you were better than the rest of us. Like you could turn your back. But I got you to come back, too."

Was that what he thought? That I saw myself as better than them? "It was more of a survival tactic to get the fuck away from you," I said.

"I should have stowed away in your trunk," Dex added.

"I know all about you," Dad said, ignoring Dex this time. It was one of his favorite digs, to pretend you didn't exist when you weren't saying anything useful to him. "My sons don't visit me in here, but the boys from the shop do. Big Jim was just here yesterday. I know you're living in the house and running the shop like a good boy. I even hear that Nora Parker's hot blonde daughter has been to the shop, sniffing around you like a bitch."

He was trying to get to me. I ignored the hot twinge of anger at the back of my neck and let a cocky grin slide onto my face. "Sure," I said. "She's all over me. She can't get enough."

Dad laughed his mean laugh, because he didn't believe it. No one believed it. "That girl wouldn't spit on you," he said, "but I'd love to see you beg for her attention. That would make my day."

"If we're done with the *Oprah* moment," Dex said, "can we discuss business so Luke and I can get the fuck out of here? This place smells like puke."

Dad scratched his chin, his face going sober as he got down to brass tacks. "Like the note said, money's dropped on the nineteenth," he said. "I made a few arrangements before I went in. The setup will run itself for a while."

"Tell us about the setup," Dex said.

"I'm not telling you anything."

But Dad's eyes betrayed him. He was worried—just a little, but it was there.

I pressed the advantage. "You don't have a choice," I said. "You're in there, and we're out here. You need us."

"I don't need you," Dad said. But it was a lie, and the lie was killing him. He hated more than anything that he needed his sons, the kids he'd treated like dirt all these years.

"You do," I said. "You had a nice little side business, but it's our business now. We get to run it."

"A *side* business?" Dad barked a laugh. "You call that kind of money a side business? You really are even stupider than I thought."

"Enlighten us," Dex said.

Dad gritted his teeth. I watched the frustration work its way through him, that he wasn't in control anymore. That for all his bluster, we were really all he had. Finally he said, "The cars come through with the others for repair. An outside driver brings them in—no one watching would know the difference. We receive them, paint them, deal with serial numbers and license plates and whatever electronic GPS shit they have, and send them out again." He looked from Dex to me. "We've been doing it at Riggs Auto for years. It's easy money, boys. All you have to do is let Big Jim handle the repairs and let the money roll in."

I felt a headache starting somewhere in the back of my neck and clawing its way upward. "And that's it?" I said. "Just hot cars?" Like years of fencing hot cars wasn't bad enough.

Dad shrugged. "It's a simple operation. Ask Jace if you don't believe me. He got me plenty of inventory before he was stupid enough to get caught."

"And where do these refurbed cars go when they leave Riggs Auto?" Dex asked.

"I don't know, and I don't care," Dad said. "I deliver them to a guy, who works for another guy, who works for another guy. No one ever introduced me to the top guy. I'm supposed to deliver cars, I deliver cars. Since I want to live past the next few weeks, I keep my mouth shut and I don't ask questions."

"And that's it?" Dex said in disbelief. "We just let Big Jim do his thing and take payment? What's your cut?"

"Fifty percent," Dad said. "You can pay my lawyer bills out of my cut and keep the rest in the safe deposit box. That's my fund for when I get out."

I laughed. "You're deluded. You're not getting out."

"You're not getting fifty percent, either," Dex said. "That's bullshit."

"That's what you think," Dad said. "Trust me, I don't plan to die in here. And when I'm out, I want my money."

Dex kicked his chair back and stood. "I'm done," he said, his voice tight. "You can stay here if you want, Luke. I'm leaving." He walked across the visiting room and out the door.

I turned to find Dad watching me. "What are you going to do, Luke?" he asked. "I left you a nice little legacy. All you have to do is let it ride."

I shook my head. Dad had never been particularly likeable, but the last eight years, plus prison, had taken him to a new level of asshole. "I don't work for you," I said.

"Wrong," Dad said as I pushed my own chair back and stood. "You do work for me. You all work for me." He kept talking as I turned my back to leave. "You think you don't want my money, Luke, but you do. You're my son. Dirty money doesn't bother you any more than it does me. And if you don't believe me, just ask your brother. Being dirty never bothered Dex one bit."

I didn't answer. But as I left, I could hear Dad laughing.

FIFTEEN

Emily

IT WAS RAINING, and it was closing time, which was my job today. The perks of being the manager. Someone had to leave early, and then someone else did too, and I was the only one who had all the keys and could close out the receipts and the booking system. And, of course, I was the only one with nowhere else to be. Pathetic.

As I was turning the lock on the front door, crouching under the small overhang over the sidewalk that kept me out of the rain, my phone rang in my purse. I dug through my bag and rummaged my phone out.

Luke.

"Hey," I said, answering a bare second before it went to voicemail.

"You finished work?" he said.

I leaned back against the locked glass door of the salon, staying out of the rain and the people going by on the sidewalk.

Luke's usual lazy drawl was gone and he sounded almost tense. "Just now," I said, pulling my summer sweater closer around me. "Why?"

"You hungry?"

At the sound of the word, my stomach clenched and grumbled. It was seven o'clock and I hadn't had any dinner yet. "Starving," I said.

"Well, I have steaks. And beer."

My stomach growled again. The Riggs house had a covered porch out back with a barbecue on it, which sounded better than pulling a Lean Cuisine out of the freezer at Mom's house while she worked late. "You grilling?" I asked him.

Luke's reply was deadpan. "Yeah. One for me, and two for you."

"Shut up, Luke."

"Em, be honest. You can pack it away like nobody's business."

Okay, fine. I had a big appetite. I always had. It wasn't sexy, but the last I heard it also wasn't a crime. "You're not supposed to mention that."

"Too late," Luke said. He was definitely tense; this wasn't much of a seduction. If that was what it was supposed to be. "Steaks and beer, Em. You in or you out?"

I was so in, but I wanted to know what this was. He'd never had me over for dinner before, or even mentioned it. This was something new. I made my voice flirtatious and said, "Perhaps. What, pray tell, happens after the steak and beer?"

"You strip," he said, "and you get on all fours on my bed. And then we'll see."

So totally, *totally* rude. And inappropriate. This was our game, the one where Luke was boss. I felt the day's tension drain away and a very happy zap of pure arousal bubbled up through my body, settling pleasantly between my legs. Anticipation, I realized. Because if it was with Luke, I would totally do that. I totally would.

I'd been on plenty of dates, in college and after. To nice restaurants, or parties, or movies. There was nothing wrong with any of them. But steak, beer, and the opportunity to get a taste of Luke's dick—for the hundredth time—gave me a buzz. I perked up, I stopped noticing the rain and my aching feet, and my breasts felt warm under my clothes. Like his hands were already on them.

I didn't know what that meant, that my body could light up this way for a guy I already knew so well. Okay, technically I knew his body more than the rest of him, because we hadn't done a lot of talking eight years ago.

But we'd done some. When you were in bed as much as Luke and I were, it was inevitable that there was at least a little bit of conversation. I knew that Luke was the calm foil to my tendency to overreact. He inexplicably got my jokes, and I always got his. I also knew he was surprisingly serious for a bad boy with a bad reputation. When I thought back on it now, it was clear to me that he hadn't taken sex lightly. Even though we were having fun, he'd never treated me like someone he could fuck and throw away. He'd taken our fun seriously, so to speak. And suddenly I had a burning question, one I'd never bothered to ask when we were eighteen. "Can I ask you something?" I said to him.

"Sure," he said, though he sounded anything but.

"When we were... together all those years ago. Did you have other girls, too? Or was there only me?"

There was a pause, long enough to make something feel hollow in my chest. Since I'd been a virgin before him, it was pretty obvious I wasn't sleeping around. And I'd just... assumed Luke wasn't. But I'd never actually *asked*.

"Em," Luke said, and his voice had tightened, become low and angry. "Sometimes you can be so fucking oblivious. Steak and beer—that's what I'm doing. You're in or you're out. Your choice." And he hung up in my ear.

He'd never done that before. It was outright rude—he'd hung up on me, in the middle of turning me on no less, and he'd called me fucking oblivious. I should be mad. I should call him back and let him have it.

But apparently I knew Luke better than I thought I did, because I also knew something else: something was wrong.

He'd invited me over for dirty sex, sure. But I realized now that he'd been trying to sweeten the pot by making me dinner. He'd invited me because he wanted company. My company. He wanted me there.

In all the time I'd known him, I'd never known him to do that. To just... ask for me to keep him company. Like a friend would.

He wanted a friend? Well, he was going to get it.

I wasn't mad. I was in.

EVEN THOUGH I had my car back and wasn't taking a taxi, I took the same precautions. I parked at the nearby strip mall and walked, even though it was raining and I didn't have an umbrella. In fact I jogged, but when I got halfway down the street, I stopped.

There was a cop car parked on the street in front of the Riggs house. No lights, no sirens, just a single black-and-white parked there, dark. I could make out the shapes of heads inside, so the cops were just in their car, sitting.

I ducked back and up behind a hedge, making my way through weeds and over a hedge behind the Riggs property, my mind racing. What the hell was going on? And how screwed up was this situation? It was possible I knew the two cops in that car, since I'd been to plenty of Mom's work functions over the years.

In fact I might have said hi to them, whoever they were, at Mom's ceremony the other night. And here I was sneaking away from them before they could see me, like I was a criminal.

I was uncomfortably wet when I got to the back of the Riggs house, my hair sticking to my forehead and my neck. I stepped up onto the covered porch and knocked on the screen door.

The door opened and Luke stood there in jeans and a tee, a plaid shirt thrown over the tee, his feet bare. He scowled at me. "What the fuck, Em?" he said.

"Did you know there are cops out front?" I asked.

He took my arm and pulled me in the house, banging the door closed behind me. "Did they see you?"

"No. What the hell are they doing here?"

He looked me up and down. "You're soaked."

"The cops would have seen an umbrella," I pointed out.

"Bullshit," Luke said. "You don't own one."

"They're annoying."

"Take your shoes off and stay there." He walked into the kitchen, which was right off the back door, and came back with a handful of tea towels. "The cops were here when I got home," he said, handing the towels to me. "I would have warned you, but I thought you weren't coming."

I scrubbed a towel over my face, another over the ends of my hair. "What do they want?"

"To scare me and to piss me off," Luke said. "I walked up to their cruiser and asked them, and they told me they're doing a security check of the neighborhood. Then they just parked and sat." He took back the wet towels and my soaked sweater, which I wadded up and handed to him. I was left wearing jeans and damp tank top. "They're here because I went to visit Dad in prison today."

I crossed my arms over my chest. "Oh Luke, I'm sorry."

He shrugged, the movement tense. "I don't think I was

followed, so I think one of the guards must have tipped the cops off."

"Why? Why do they care if you visit your father in prison?"

"Dad is into some serious shit, and he's dropped me in the middle of it. With Dad in jail, it looks like I'm the new punching bag." He blinked, probably remembering he was talking about the Westlake PD. "Sorry."

I sighed and pushed my damp hair from my face. This was such a mess. "You said you have beer."

He led me into the kitchen, where I took a seat on one of the breakfast stools. There was a basic single guy's dinner layout happening: steaks in butcher paper, salt and pepper, a fresh loaf of bread, a six pack of beer. Nothing fancy, and no vegetables. My mouth watered.

Luke picked up the steaks in paper and grabbed a pair of barbecue tongs. "I'll be right back."

He put the steaks on the grill and came back through the screen door. I opened my beer and watched him, I hoped covertly. I'd never seen Luke in a kitchen before. He looked ridiculously good, of course. He wasn't wearing a ball cap, and his dark hair was mussed. He hadn't had a haircut in a while, and with the wet weather he had curls. With the dark scruff on his jaw and his amazing body, he was quietly spectacular. If I wasn't so hungry, and craving steak, I'd probably skip straight to the naked part if he'd let me.

He didn't seem to notice. He washed his hands in the sink, the cuffs of his shirt pushed halfway up his forearms. "So I take it the answer to my question was no," I said to him.

He shut off the water. "What?"

"My question from before. About whether you had other girls when we were seeing each other before."

He shrugged and dried his hands, not looking at me. "You really need it spelled out? No."

I ignored the relief that warmed my chest. "You could have just said that."

"I'm in a pissy mood."

I could see that. Visiting your father in prison, then coming home to find cops parked in front of your house, would put most people in a pissy mood. "Okay, it was kind of a dumb question. I just realized I never asked it."

He dropped the towel on the counter and braced himself on his arms, looking at me. "Is that what you're asking about now?" he said. "You want exclusivity?"

His look was a little wild—he really wasn't in a very good mood. Still, his question was so absurd that I laughed, which would probably poke the beast. "Luke Riggs," I said, "if you're fucking some other woman right now, you're never getting in my pants again. Ever."

"And who would I be fucking?" Luke said. "The woman who runs the gas station and has no teeth? Or the women on the other side of the tracks, who look at me like I'm dogshit?"

That sobered me a little. "You're sort of good-looking, Luke," I said. "Women like you."

"They just don't like to admit it," he shot back. "Face it, Em, I'm a Riggs. That's all I'll ever be." He walked to the door again, going outside to flip the steaks.

I'd never seen him like this, prickly and spoiling for a fight, but for some reason it didn't bother me. I almost liked it. It was honest, the real Luke. Seeing his father had obviously upset him, and with good reason, so I saw no reason for him to push those feelings down and cover them up. I was the last person to give advice about suppressing your feelings.

So even though he was mad, I just slid off my chair, found a bread knife, and sliced up the bread while he grilled. I pulled out plates and even found steak knives in a drawer—they weren't part of a set, but they would do. I found a roll of paper towels we could use for napkins, and a small sliver of butter in the fridge. When Luke came back in to get the salt and pepper, I handed him an opened beer.

"Thanks," he grumbled and left again.

I let him simmer it off until the steaks were on plates, along with fresh bread and butter. We sat at the stools at the counter, not bothering with the kitchen table, which was covered in unopened mail. "You want to talk about it?" I asked when we had dug in.

He shrugged, but the flash of anger had gone. "My father is an asshole," he said. "So is my brother."

"Which one?"

That got me the ghost of a smile. "Dex," he replied. "Dex is an asshole."

I cut another bite of steak. It was delicious. "You went on this little trip with Dex?"

Luke put his fork down and massaged the spot between his eyes as if he was in pain. "Yes," he said. He didn't elaborate.

"Do you want to tell me about it?"

"No."

Okay then. If he wasn't going to talk about the fact that he might be running his father's stolen car business, then neither was I. I took another bite. "So the whole trip was already awful, and then you came home and found cops at the end of your driveway. And all of it sucked so much that you called me."

He was still massaging the spot between his eyes. "Something like that."

"It was a sex call," I said, gesturing with my fork, "and yet it wasn't. I figured that out after you hung up. I'm a little slow sometimes, Luke, but I do catch on."

He dropped his hand and opened his eyes. "Catch on to what?"

"You wanted company," I said. "You wanted me to come over and hang out. The sex was just the icing on the cake."

His gaze went dark, flickered down me and up again. My tank top was damp, and so was my hair. I had no idea what my makeup looked like, but it probably wasn't good. I was also stuffing my face with food, but he said, "Em, sex is not the icing on the cake with you. Ever."

My body gave a happy little shiver at that: *Okay then! That's all I need! Let's do this!* But I shushed it and said, "You wanted to talk to me. Admit it."

He was quiet for a minute. He picked up his bread and pulled it apart in his big hands, his gaze trained on it instead of on me. "It bothers me," he said slowly and clearly, "that I never got to take you on a date."

I nearly dropped my fork, I was so shocked. "What?"

"A date," Luke said again. He put the bread down. "I never got to take you on one. I always thought you were the kind of woman who would like that. Get dressed up, go somewhere nice. I never got to do that." He sat back in his chair, looked at the meal in front of us. "This was the best I could do."

I just stared at him, frozen. I was honestly so surprised that I was absolutely speechless. A date? That's what this was? A date?

An hour ago, I'd been thinking that I'd never been on a date that was all that special. Why was it that when Luke mentioned a date, I felt like sweeping all the dishes aside in a big movie moment and jumping into his lap?

"What?" he said, frowning. I'd been quiet too long.

"That—" I found my voice. "That's the nicest thing you've ever said to me." I paused. "That's the nicest thing *anyone* has ever said to me."

He rolled his eyes, but his skin was a little flushed. "You're being dramatic again."

I took a swig of my beer, still watching him. God, he was

adorable. "I don't put out on dates," I told him. "That's why Trevor Halbersen dumped me in high school, remember?"

"His loss was my gain," Luke said.

"And college..." I sighed. "College sex was so *complicated*. Everyone is stuck between high school and actual adulthood. No one knows if they're just having fun or trying to find The One and settle down. Some people are getting married and having babies already, and some are just screwing around, and everyone else is in the middle somewhere, and you never know whether the other person is going to try and marry you or dump you in an hour."

"Yeah?" Luke dug back into his steak. "Anyone try and marry you, Parker?"

"No." I watched his face carefully, but it was impossible to read. "No one was that serious." Still nothing. I poked the bear further, because I could never help it. "I don't know why, really. I'm the whole package—looks, brains, killer body. Someone should have definitely tried to put a ring on it."

He was amused now, which made me relax. I was pulling him out of his tense mood. "You think?" he said.

"Sure," I said. "My theory is that most men are intimidated by me. One guy broke up with me because he said he felt like he was disappointing me all the time."

Luke actually laughed at that, a low sound that thrilled me because it was so rare. "Jesus, Em, what did you do to these guys?"

I didn't know how to answer that. I *had* been hard on the guys I'd dated. I'd expected a lot—everything, really. I'd expected easy conversation and anticipation and mind-blowing sex and physical closeness that was effortless and thrilling at the same time. I'd expected a wild zing every time a man put his hands on me, a fizzle of tension that never quit. I expected orgasms that made me forget everything else in life, put me in the moment and made life fun.

Like with Luke.

I had gone off to college expecting every guy to be like Luke. And I'd been terribly, horribly wrong.

But I didn't want to say any of that, so instead I said, "They didn't hire me at my last internship because I wasn't nice enough."

That surprised him, his dark eyes rising to mine. "What?"

"They gave me a performance review and said I didn't smile enough. They said I had too many opinions and I talked too much at meetings. So they didn't give me a job."

The burn of it was, they were right. I had done all of those things. It wasn't that I thought I knew everything, or that I was trying to show off. I was just me. I put myself out there, said too much. And in the corporate world, that was a total embarrassment. Interns were supposed to shut up and look nice and get coffee.

I should have read that, should have obeyed the unwritten rules. Should have changed myself to get that job. But I hadn't managed even that much, even with my career on the line.

"That's bullshit, Em," Luke said. "You don't want to work for a place like that."

I blinked at him. "I failed, Luke."

He shrugged. "You failed at being a corporate suit. So what?" He gave me the ghost of a smile, wry and a little sad. "You're a good girl, Emily, but you've never been *that* good."

Because I'd been with him, he meant. No girl who was *that* good would be with him.

No girl who was *that* good would be with him right now, while cops were parked at the end of his driveway, staking out his father's stolen car operation.

I had that feeling again, that unease in my stomach. This was the way of things, right? I was good, and Luke wasn't. Except no one who thought they knew Luke Riggs saw the guy I was sitting across from right now.

And I *hadn't* been happy in that internship. I'd gone to college, and I'd worked so hard, and I'd thought I'd be a CEO. And instead, I hadn't liked the corporate world at all. If I'd gotten that job, I'd have a paycheck right now, but I knew in my gut that I'd also be miserable.

Something shifted inside me, cracked a little. I hadn't let myself think about Luke in eight years. I hadn't let myself miss him. Because I did. And I had. Being with him now, with the guy who'd been my first and had actually gone to the trouble to make it good, was like opening a door I'd closed a long time ago. Things were neater with the door closed, but there was a whole room you couldn't see.

I wanted to kiss him. Just the way he did it, with his mouth making me crazy and his hands on my skin. He always gave me his full attention when he kissed me, like no other woman ever existed. He'd go slow or fast, go deep with his tongue or drop lazy kisses along the edge of my mouth. Luke could kiss for hours without sex—I knew from experience, the nights we'd made out when I was still a virgin. That was one thing I knew about Luke Riggs: he was a champion, world-class kisser, the best of the best.

Had he kissed other women like that? I didn't know, and right now I didn't care. It was me he'd called tonight, me who was sitting here with him while the rain lashed the windows. Me who he'd tried to give a real date to. I'd known him for so long, and we'd done so much, but it turned out Luke and I had unfinished business.

I wanted to finish it. I had to.

Even if, in the end, it would wreck both of us.

SIXTEEN

Emily

AFTER DINNER, with the sky dark and the rain still coming down, the police car was still there. I found Luke standing in the living room at the front of the house, in the dark, watching the parked car through a gap in the curtains.

"They aren't going to leave," he said softly when he heard me behind him. He didn't turn around.

Even in the dark, without touching him, I could see the tension in his shoulders, the hard way he held himself, the clamped-down line of his jaw. This was what he'd come home to: cops dogging his every move, courtesy of Mike Riggs.

Maybe he deserved it. I had no idea.

I put a hand on his arm, feeling the hard granite of his bicep under his shirt. "Did you know?" I asked him softly.

He paused, then gave a quick shake of his head, so subtle you would miss it if you weren't watching like I was. "He wasn't into that shit when I left. Not that I knew of, anyway. And when I came back..." He shoved his hands in his pockets, still looking out the window at the darkened police car. "It didn't surprise me. It didn't surprise any of us. We just don't know what to fucking do."

I stepped closer to him, my breasts brushing his back, my hand curling up over his shoulder. He nearly flinched beneath my touch, and I wondered if anyone had ever comforted Luke, ever bothered to make sure he was okay. "There's nothing you can do tonight," I whispered, resting my chin on his shoulder. "Let them sit there in the rain if they want to. Let's go."

He didn't move, but when I moved my hand down and hooked it gently in his belt, he turned and followed me. Up the stairs, down the darkened hall to his bedroom.

I pulled my tank top off, so I was wearing only my lacy bra. I tugged off his shirt, then his T-shirt, pulling it over his head and dropping it on the floor. The game wasn't going to be played tonight, after all; I didn't want to, and I sensed neither did he. What I wanted tonight was something else.

He cupped my face, moving his thumb along the line of my jaw, but I didn't kiss him, even though I wanted to. Instead I dragged my hands down his chest and his stomach. I unbuckled his belt, worked open his jeans, and sank to my knees.

Luke groaned, a soft sound almost of pain, but he didn't stop me. I settled on my knees and pulled his cock out, pumping it twice, admiring it. Then I put my mouth on it, and I wasn't shy. I put it all the way in.

He felt good. He tasted good. Luke was the first guy I'd ever done this to—one of the things we'd experimented with that summer, practicing until I learned to like it. And I had. Before I'd ever tried it I thought the act might be demeaning, but the reality was different. The reality was that Luke fucking *loved* this, and while I was doing it I owned him body and soul.

I took him deep, bracing my palms on his thighs, and he groaned again, this time deep in his throat. "Em," he said, his voice ragged. I felt his hands in my hair, not pushing me but stroking my hair back from my face, twisting it gently in his grip. He was watching me, I knew. Giving himself a clearer view.

I took it slow and easy. All the way in, and all the way out again, sucking the tip. Then all the way in. His hands tightened in my hair and his thighs were hard beneath my hands, and I got lost in it, my eyes closed, my heart racing. I could smell him, how aroused he was. I could hear his ragged breathing. He sometimes used to talk to me while I did this, say dirty things, but this time he said nothing. I seemed to have rendered him speechless.

I kept at it, a slow and easy pace because I didn't want him to come too fast. My nipples were hard in my lacy bra, and I was so wet between my legs it was almost uncomfortable. I pulled him from my mouth and put my hand on him, squeezing him gently while I licked the tip, the blood pounding between my legs, and that was when his hands left my hair and he pulled me up.

I was tossed on my back on the bed. He loomed over me, his eyes dark and wild, his jeans undone, that dark tat winding down his muscled arm. He put a hand on my belly and hooked his fingers under the waist of my jeans.

"Eight years, Em," he said in that ragged voice, his eyes never leaving me. "Eight years I pictured your mouth on my cock every time another woman did that."

Lust and anger bubbled under my skin, and I punched him on the shoulder, just above his pec. "Fuck you," I said. Fuck him for mentioning another woman here, now. My voice cracked, which made me mad, so I punched him again, harder.

He didn't even flinch, didn't move away. His skin was hot where I hit him, the muscles hard. "Yeah," he said, his voice harsh with something I recognized as pain. "I fucked other women. What was I supposed to do? You went off to your life, your future, and the only thing I could think of to do was get in my car and keep driving." He undid my jeans and slid them down my hips, along with my panties. I didn't stop him. I just lay there watching him, mesmerized. "I'd picture you in college somewhere, fucking some college guy. Coming like you did with me. Maybe telling him you loved him. Maybe wanting to marry him. And I'd go find some woman and fuck her, and you know what? It was never you."

"Luke," I said, my voice cracking again, this time not with anger.

He pulled my jeans off my legs, tossed them away. "I'd get in my car and go somewhere else," he said, the words ripping out of him like they hurt. "But wherever I went, I'd picture the same thing. And I'd do it again. You want to know how the story ends? It wasn't you there either." He braced himself on his arms and leaned over me. "It was never you. That's what I had to figure out. It was never going to be you. Not ever again."

Was *this* how he felt? It was killing me—it was breaking me open. "Baby, come here," I said, cupping my hands on his rough jaw. "Come here."

But he took his jeans and boxer briefs off, then reached into his nightstand and took a condom out of the box. "We'll never work, Em," he said, ripping open the wrapper and rolling the condom onto his big, thick cock, his eyes on me. "We never have. We can't even have a cup of coffee together."

He was right, but screw that. Screw all of it. I raised my feet and put one on each of his bare shoulders. "Come here," I said again.

Still watching me, Luke changed position, moving forward, coming over top of me, braced straight on his arms. As he moved my body bent, opening me to him with my ankles on his shoulders, vulnerable and wet. He moved his muscled hips and slid inside me, the position making it so deep that I cried out.

"Fuck," he said, moving his hips again and going even deeper. He was all the way inside me, filling me to the point of pain, and I loved it. I arched my back and tried to get him even deeper.

He pulled out and thrust in again, harder this time, and I cried out again, not even bothering to be quiet. "Oh, my *god.*"

His voice was low and tight as he withdrew again, one of his big hands on my knee. "You are so fucking hot," he said, and thrust into me again, hard.

I cried out yet again, in time with every thrust. Maybe the cops could hear us from the road—I didn't care. "Do that more, Luke," I said. "God, yes. Do that more."

He pressed into me. My body was entirely his, entirely open, his possession. "Christ, Em," he said hoarsely in my ear. "You take me so deep, and you always fucking love it."

"More," I moaned.

His hand took mine and pushed it down between my legs. His fingers stayed on mine and we both stroked me over and over as he fucked me deep. We'd had raunchy teenaged sex all those years ago, in every position, but that was different from this. It had been an exploration, a game. This was serious—Luke Riggs was a man, a beast, and he was fucking me as hard as he could.

And I came. The orgasm shuddered through me, starting deep and blowing outward, and I let it take over, let myself go. It was so intense I could barely breathe, and I had no idea what sounds I made. It didn't matter. Luke stroked me through it, his hand still over mine, both of us stroking me until he went still and came, deep inside me. When he was finished he pulled my ankles from his shoulders, though I wrapped my legs around his waist instead, unwilling to let him go.

He braced himself on his elbows over me and lowered his forehead to the side of my neck. "I think you're going to kill me," he said after a minute.

I still didn't let him go. I liked him exactly where he was, his big body over mine, between my legs, his cock still inside me. We were meant to be like this, him and me. It was like our bodies had been made to interlock.

I wrapped my arms around his neck, ran my fingers through the soft messy curls of his hair, ran my lips over the rough beautiful line of his jaw. He stayed still, letting me do what I wanted. Had anyone ever poured affection on him? Well, I was doing it now.

"Luke," I said against his skin, "I've decided something."

There was a flicker in the muscles beneath my touch, a flinch. Like he thought whatever I was going to say was going to be bad. And I realized that in his quiet way, this was how Luke worked. He figured things would be bad, and he braced for it.

Maybe what I was going to say was bad. I still didn't know. But I was saying it anyway.

I leaned into his ear. I kissed the warm skin beneath it. And then I said, "We're not over. And we never will be."

SEVENTEEN

Luke

DAD WAS RIGHT. The stolen cars were brought in mixed with the legitimate ones, by a nondescript guy who tossed Big Jim the keys, got into a waiting car with a buddy behind the wheel, and drove away again. The guy, whoever he was, was at Riggs Auto for sixty seconds tops.

I'd figured out the pattern by now. The car I was standing in front of was your basic Honda SUV, two or three years old, silver gray. A ton of them on the street. Not distinctive. A car used to drive kids around, maybe, or a car for some guy to drive out of the city and to his cottage in the summer.

"Where the fuck do they get them?" I asked Big Jim, who was standing next to me. Both of us were in garage coveralls. I had my arms crossed over my chest, and Big Jim was sitting on an empty metal crate, smoking a cigarette. No one really bothered with smoking rules at Riggs.

"All kinds of places," Big Jim said. "Mall parking lots. Long-term lots at the airport are good places, because no one knows the thing has been gone for days, sometimes weeks. Parking garages were your brother Jace's specialty. He could nab just the right vehicle from a parking garage—knew all the cameras' blind spots. Fucking ninja, that kid." He shook his head and took a drag on his cigarette.

I didn't think Jace would be happy to hear how admired he was for his car-stealing skills. I glanced toward the front where the windows were. I'd seen a cop car drive by twice today, going nice and slow, on a lookout. Nora Parker's cops wanted us to know they were watching.

"This is dangerous," I said to Big Jim. "We've got heat, thanks to Dad."

"Mike did screw things up royally," Big Jim said, dropping his smoke to the ground and stepping on it. "But I put my kid through college on this money. This business isn't going anywhere, son."

I walked around the SUV. Looked in the windows. It was in good shape, barely a scratch on it. "There are bags in the back seat," I said.

"Just a bonus," Big Jim replied. "Woman leaves her shopping bags in the car, the car gets stolen, Merry Christmas to us. The people we pass the car on to don't want it. It's ours."

"So we take their stuff, too?"

Big Jim laughed softly. "You're not used to this shit, are you, kid?"

I didn't look at him.

"Jace had a problem with that too," the big man said. "He'd toss the stuff out before he'd jack the car. It became kind of his trademark, so to speak. But to answer your question, yeah, we steal their stuff. We've found everything from wallets to jewelry. It's easy money, man. Jackpot."

I circled the SUV, my eyes still on it.

"I'm sure Mike told you we answer to some pretty big people," Jim said. "People you don't want to fuck with."

"Yeah," I said.

"Those people want to keep this operation going, even without Mike. In fact, I'd say they insist on it."

I raised my eyes to him for the first time, looked at him from beneath the brim of my baseball cap. "You think I'm planning to shut this down?"

Big Jim scratched his gray beard. "I think you're thinking about it," he said. "I also think it's a stupid idea to think about it."

"I didn't say I was thinking about it."

He shrugged, tried a grin. "You're an open book, kid."

"You don't know anything about me," I told him. "Not one fucking thing."

He sobered, but his eyes went beady with annoyance. "I know you used to be a punk-ass kid with no brains and a bad attitude."

"Yeah, well, a long time ago you were in diapers, Big Jim. Doesn't make a difference to the man you are now."

Big Jim stood up, brushed his oily hands over his coveralls like he was dusting off dirt. "You saying you're a big enough man to handle the business now?"

"I'm saying that if we play it stupid and the cops shut us down, we'll all be inside with dear old Dad. And no one will be making any money anymore. Bye bye, college tuition."

It was Big Jim's turn to cross his arms over his chest. It was a big chest. He was a big guy. "What are you gonna do about it?" he said.

That was the question. Because it was the nineteenth, and when I'd gone into the safe out back this morning I'd found a plastic grocery bag inside. It was full of money. We didn't have security cameras anywhere at Riggs—the idea of Dad putting in something like that was laughable—so I checked the alarm code record. Someone had keyed in the alarm code at two thirty-seven a.m., then armed it again at two forty-three. The money drop was a six-minute job.

I assumed Big Jim, and a few others, got similar deliveries. Unfuckingbelievable.

I was a Riggs. Mike Riggs' son. I was never going to go to college or be a rich man. I was never going to own one of the big houses on the other side of the Westlake tracks and send my kids to the best schools. I was never going to travel the world or make scientific discoveries. I was going to stay right here in Westlake, in my father's house. I was going to drive my Charger, and if I was lucky I would avoid knocking up Mindy Green, who lived down the street and already had two kids by two different guys. I'd find some washed-out woman to marry me someday and we'd live from paycheck to paycheck in semi-contentment. If we were lucky.

We're not done, Emily Parker said in my head, *and we never will be.*

I'd thought of nothing but Emily for days. Nothing but this shit that went around and around in my head. Because that last night we'd been together had changed things for me. It had made me realize that the woman I wanted, the woman I'd always wanted, was Emily Parker. I wanted her body and I wanted her mind and I wanted her laugh and I wanted every bitchy, prickly thing that came out of her mouth. I wanted the way she rode me and the way she milked my cock and the way she didn't think I was scum. I wanted the way she looked at me like I was human instead of *one of those Riggs boys who'd never amount to anything.*

I shouldn't want any of those things. Because I *was* one of those Riggs boys. I lived in the real world. The world where I wasn't going to get what I wanted.

I had spent eight years running away from this problem, and it had only chased me all the way home.

You've got a problem here, Riggs. Man up.

This problem—the stolen car problem—was tied up with the Emily problem. Not just the fact that her mother was the one who could put me away. It was because both problems left me with the same question: *Man up, Riggs. What are you going to do?*

"Fix it," I said aloud to Big Jim. "I'm going to fix it."

"The cops won't take a payoff," he said. "We tried that. That bitch Nora Parker has the force by the balls. Every one of those guys is locked down tight."

"You think she's a bitch?" I asked.

"Actually I think she's a cunt, but bitch will do," he replied.

I exhaled a breath. These were the guys I worked with. These guys worked *for* me. Riggs Auto was mine, and these were the guys I would always work with. This was the kind of guy I would someday be.

Did I have to be? Dad had taught me nothing, and I'd had no role models, no nice teachers or coaches who taught me how to be a man. My brothers were no help, because they had the same problem. Now Jace was a con, Ryan had knocked a girl up and torpedoed his baseball career, and Dex was barely conscious. This is what happens when the boys on the wrong side of the tracks are raised like a litter of feral puppies.

The only person who had been good to me was Emily. We'd been secret and we'd been dirty, and I'd never been someone she could be seen in public with, but that didn't change the fact that she'd been nice. She'd trusted me—enough to let me take her virginity, which for Emily had been a big fucking deal. She hadn't pitied or despised me, and she'd wanted to be around me. I'd always known it was temporary, that she would leave, so when it happened I thought I was fine with it.

But I'd spent eight years on the road, not wanting anything:

not a home, not a permanent job, not a relationship with a woman. I'd done that because it was easier and safer not to want something in the first place, than to want it and never have it. I did it because, I realized now, the only thing I'd wanted had never been mine. So why want anything at all?

We're not done, and we never will be.

What had started out as some dirty fun had turned into something I didn't expect: a chance. A shot. Maybe. If I was willing to take it.

"I'm going to fix it," I said again.

Big Jim sounded worried. He probably saw his college tuition spiraling the drain. "I don't think you can, man."

He was wrong, though. The cops were one problem; the criminals were another. I could fix both of them.

And my brothers were going to help me.

"NO," Ryan said on the phone. "I'm not doing it. No way."

"You'll do it," I told him. "Jace is already in."

"Bullshit, Luke. You're lying."

Shit. I was. I hadn't even asked Jace yet. I was counting on Ryan, because he was better at persuading the other two than I was. "Okay fine, I'm lying. But Jace will totally be in."

"Yeah, right," Ryan said. "And Dex?"

"Dex will be in once you talk to him."

Ryan sighed. "Dude, put that down."

"What?"

"I was talking to Dylan. No, I mean all the way down, not just in your lap. Still not down, man."

I waited.

"Okay," Ryan said, presumably to me again. "What were we talking about? Oh right, your batshit idea."

"You're saying shit in front of a kid again."

"Thanks, dad of the year. I'm still not in."

"Then you're in the same trouble the rest of us are. Because we've got a week, maybe two max before this blows up and we all go to jail."

"I didn't do anything," Ryan said. "I'm all the way here in Detroit."

"You take that money from Dad?"

Ryan was quiet.

"The minute we went to the bank and found that money without calling the cops, we were part of this," I said. "All of us."

"Fuck, I haven't touched the money," Ryan said. "It's sitting in a drawer. I can hardly look at it. I thought I'd be able to spend it, but damn." He was caving. He knew the same thing I did: any risk, no matter how small, was too much risk. Especially for a guy who was the only thing a seven-year-old kid had in the world.

"Then we do this," I said, "or you can find someone else to raise Dylan while you go away."

"Fuck you, Luke."

Now he was saying fuck in front of his kid, but this time I refrained from pointing it out. He was right, I was probably the worst guy for fatherly advice. Except for Dex, maybe. Dex was worse.

"Tomorrow night," I said. "Are you in or are you out?"

Ryan groaned. "Fine, I'm in. Let me call the nanny and see if she can watch Dylan."

"There's a nanny?" I asked.

"Of course there's a nanny. I've got training and practice and therapy, I can't pick him up from school every day. Apparently real parents pick their kids up from school. Who knew?"

"Not me," I said. If any of us had mentioned being picked up from school, Dad would have laughed in our faces.

"Me neither," Ryan said.

"Is the nanny hot?" I asked.

I was just trying to goad him—it was second nature—but Ryan paused carefully. "The nanny is a very nice woman," he said.

I laughed. Suddenly my foul-mouthed brother was speaking as carefully as a kindergarten teacher with his kid in the room. "So she is hot."

"She has excellent references and does a good job," was the speech I got in reply. "She takes good care of Dylan, who is sitting next to me right now."

"And you're definitely not sleeping with her," I said. "The nanny."

"That is an activity that we haven't discussed."

"Yet."

"It's unlikely to happen," Ryan said. "It probably isn't a good idea."

"So let me get this straight," I said. I was enjoying this. "You're stuck with a hot nanny working for you every day, and you can't lay a hand on her."

His voice was still careful. "That's pretty accurate, yes."

"Well, call the hot nanny and ask if she's free tomorrow night. And after that, call Dex. I'll take care of Jace."

"Go to hell, Luke," Ryan said, and he hung up. But he'd do it. I already knew he would.

I called Jace next. He heard me out, and then to my surprise he agreed. *I'm in,* he said. But he'd have to take the bus from Detroit. I needed to get my brother a damn car.

I hung up with Jace, and with all of that over, I finally called the one voice I actually wanted to hear, the voice I'd been thinking of all day. I flipped through my numbers and called Emily.

EIGHTEEN

Emily

WESTLAKE WAS quiet at three o'clock in the morning. I pulled up in Mom's driveway and got out of the car as quietly as I could, trying not to slam the door. I turned the key in the front door silently and slipped into the house, pushing off my sandals as soon as I was inside.

I was tiptoeing down the hall toward the stairs when I saw the figure in the kitchen.

Mom was sitting at the kitchen table in a bathrobe. In front of her was a steaming cup of tea. The little lamp in the phone nook —yeah, we had a phone nook—was on, the warm glow lighting her face as she looked at me. "Have a seat," she said, using her foot to push out the chair opposite her.

The first thing I felt was a rush of guilt. Old habits die hard. Then I remembered to give myself a little dignity. I kept my chin up as I walked to the kitchen table and sat down.

Mom looked at me for a long minute, her gaze going up and

down me. There was no way around it: I was completely sex-disheveled. My hair was tousled, my bra was in my purse, my makeup was gone, and my lips were raw.

I'd gone to Luke's again tonight. I hadn't been able to stay away; I'd wanted to see him more than anything. I'd gone to his back door again, in case the cops drove by out front. We hadn't had dinner this time, because we'd both been in the same mood: intense, impatient, and burning up.

He'd gone down on me right there in the kitchen, pushing my dress up and pulling my panties down, licking me as I leaned back against the kitchen counter. After I came, he turned me and bent me over that same counter, his cock big and harsh inside me as he said dirty things in my ear. He'd pounded me hard until we both came, sweating and panting, but we hadn't even exchanged a word before we were upstairs in his bed and I was riding him, taking his cock inside me again, unable to get enough. We'd both come again, and then we'd dozed for a while, and then he'd fucked me one last time before I left, pressing me facedown into the bed and pulling my legs open while his hands and his cock sent me into oblivion.

In short, we'd fucked and fucked and fucked, and it was glorious, and it was written all over me. For my mother to see.

"Honey," she said.

"Mom." My voice was a rasp from shouting so much at Luke's place. "I'm twenty-six."

"I know," she said. I watched her face, listened to her tone carefully, and I didn't see any disapproval there. Instead, what I saw was concern, unmixed with anything else. She was worried about me.

I stared down at the table and said nothing. Why was she worried about me? I'd never given her reason to be. I wasn't wild. I wasn't even slutty, even though that wasn't really a thing. But having my mother look at me like that made me automatically wonder what I was doing wrong.

"Does he treat you nicely?" Mom said into the quiet. "Whoever he is?"

I looked up at her again. Was she kidding? This was Luke we were talking about, even though she didn't know it. "Yeah, he does," I said.

Mom sighed. Her hair was down, and even tired as she was in the middle of the night, I knew she was a good-looking woman. Dad had been a looker, too, when they married. Lauren and I were blessed in the genetics department. "I always hoped you would find someone," she said.

I frowned. "What do you mean?"

"You're an independent spirit," Mom said. "You always have been. You were never one of those girls who was looking for romance all the time. Do you think I didn't notice?" She smiled. "You had a few boyfriends in high school, but none of them took. Then, after the Halbersen boy, you stopped dating altogether until you left for college. And you didn't seem to miss it at all."

I stared at her. She was talking about the period I'd been with Luke. When no one had known. Mom had thought I was single the whole time.

"College was the same," Mom went on. "You told us about a few dates here and there, but you never brought anyone home. You never seemed serious with anyone."

"I wasn't," I said.

Mom nodded. "You're young, and you have lots of time. But I'm your mother, and sometimes I wondered if maybe you were alone too much. It's a silly sentimental thing, I know, but I've always wanted to see you fall in love. With someone great, of course. Someone worthy of you."

I could feel that my jaw had dropped. I remembered to close

my mouth. I'd never had a conversation like this with my mother in my life. I had no idea what to say.

Mom smiled. "And here you are," she said.

She meant love. That was what she thought. "It was just sex," I said, the words automatic, but even as they came out of my mouth they tasted bad. Sure, Luke and I had just banged like it was our mission in life, but right now I was so freaking happy I was walking on a cloud of bliss. I was addicted. I wanted to do that every night, anytime I wanted, and only with Luke. He was *mine*. That was what I wanted: all of him. For all of him to be mine.

That wasn't just sex, and never had been.

Mom shook her head, like she was reading my mind. "That's what I mean," she said. "You don't just have sex. You never have. You're choosy. And honey, the look on your face right now. I've known you since the minute you were born, and I don't think I've ever seen you happy like this." She reached out and touched my wrist. "I like him, whoever he is."

I blinked hard. *He's Luke Riggs,* I wanted to say. The words were so close they were floating in the back of my throat. *He's Luke Riggs, and all my life you've told me to stay away from him because he isn't good enough for me. But he is. He's the only one who is.*

"I'm not going to pry," Mom said, letting go of my wrist and sitting back. "And I know I look like the disapproving parent, sitting up for you in the middle of the night. But you've come home late like this a few times now, and I wanted you to know I know. And that when you're ready, I really do want to meet him."

She got up and left, putting her empty tea mug on the counter. I sat in the warm light from the phone nook, feeling like something big had happened. Something major.

I heard Mom's bedroom door close, and after more time

passed in silence I knew she was probably asleep. And still I sat there, alone, my mind reeling.

Damn it. Damn it. I was so stupid. It was just hitting me now.

Mom thought I'd never been in love, but she was wrong. I was picky because I *had* been in love.

I was in love with Luke Riggs, and part of me always had been.

NINETEEN

Luke

FRIDAY NIGHT IN WESTLAKE, when it wasn't football season, was never all that wild. There were a few places on the downtown strip that had their regulars: the Fire Pit, which didn't serve alcohol, for the high schoolers; the Irish Brogue for the middle aged drinkers (though there was barely a drop of Irish blood anywhere in Westlake); the White Martini which pretended to be a dance bar/hookup spot and was mostly just gross. And, at the end of the strip, a rundown place called the Barn, where the hardcore, don't-fuck-with-me drinkers went.

Ronny Red was one of those don't-fuck-with-me drinkers, especially since Dad had tried to run him over. He was sitting at the Barn's greasy bar, drinking beer from a none-too-clean glass, breathing the sweaty air and staring at nothing. Until I came through the door, and then he was staring at me.

His eyes went wide, and he shifted on his stool. Ronny was about fifty, with sparse hair and a face that showed years of hard drinking. He was wearing old army pants and a stained T-shirt, and he had a medical boot on one foot.

I walked toward him, not looking left or right. "Ronny," I said.

He put down his beer and hopped off his stool. "Gotta go," he said to the bartender, and he hobbled away from me, across the dim room toward the back door.

"Ronny," I said, following him, "you don't go very fast."

"Fuck off, Luke Riggs."

I kept following him, taking my time.

"I said fuck off," Ronny said again. I didn't touch him—I had no intention to—but it didn't escape me that exactly none of the other people in the Barn, including the bartender, came to Ronny's rescue or said a word. They just let me herd him out the back door while they sipped their beers.

"I got nothing to say to you," Ronny shouted back over his shoulder as he stumped down the rear hallway and pushed open the back door. "You just stay away from me, Luke."

"What about me?" Ryan said. He was standing right outside the Barn's back door, legs apart and arms crossed. Behind him was his car, the big showy black SUV. He had a smirk on his lips, because he was enjoying this. "You want me to stay away?"

Ronny stopped short when he saw Ryan, then swiveled left. "I'll call the cops," he said, wiping sweat from his lip. "See if I don't. You Riggs boys are crazy."

"No, we're not." Jace came out of the shadows, herding Ronny back toward the SUV. "That's just Dex."

"Yeah, I am," Dex agreed. He was standing by the driver's door. "Get in the car, Ronny. We just want to talk."

Ronny looked at us standing in a circle around him. Four on one was overkill, maybe, but we wanted to get the message across. If I'd approached Ronny alone, he would have run to his car and driven away without another word. Ronny was a chicken, but he could be mean when cornered. You had to have a show of force to make him obey.

Besides, we weren't going to beat him up. That I knew of.

"Seriously, man, just get in the car," I said.

Ronny caved. He hobbled toward the SUV, where Jace herded him into the back seat. Then Jace got in one side of him, I got on the other, Ryan got in the passenger side, and Dex got behind the wheel. He started the SUV and pulled out onto Winchester Street.

"What's this about?" Ronny said.

Ryan's SUV was big, but I was still too close to Ronny in this back seat, my leg touching his. It was unpleasant, to say the least. "We have some questions," I said.

"I don't know what about. Mike already tried to kill me. I just want you to leave me alone."

In the front seat, Dex said to Ryan, "You know what they say about SUV's like this? They're a cover for your tiny dick."

"Shut up, Dex," Ryan said. "Why the hell are you driving, anyway? You're probably high as a kite."

"Because I'm the oldest."

"Yeah, well, scratch my car and you'll be dead. Then I'll be the oldest."

I shut my eyes for a second. Jesus. "Guys, we're in the middle of something here."

"Right," Ryan said. "How have you been, Ronny Red?"

"Not so good," Ronny said. He smelled like stale beer and desperation. "My ankle and all."

"Yeah, that's too bad," Dex said. "Pretty rude of Dad to mess you up like that. But I guess he's paying the price."

Ronny twitched in his seat. "I didn't send him to prison, man. I didn't even call the cops. It was the waitress at the Barn who did it. She saw the whole thing. I would have worked it out with Mike, man to man."

He thought we were coming for revenge. Like we gave a shit that Dad was locked up. "What we want to know is why," I told him. "Why did he try to run you over?"

Ronny looked at his lap and said nothing.

"Just tell us," I said.

"I don't remember. Mike was drunk. He was just mad, that's all."

"Ryan," Dex said in the front seat, "you remember the route to the old quarry? No one there this time of night."

"True," Ryan said. "You take Line Five, just to the right up here. The turnoff is hard to see in the dark."

"Right, I remember. Ronny, let's take a trip."

"Don't," Ronny said. He was really scared now. Dex had that effect on people. In fact, even I wasn't sure if he'd drive us out to the old quarry in the dark. And if he did, what he'd do with Ronny once we got there.

"Just tell us," I said to him again. "Why did Dad run you over?"

Ronny sighed and wiped his sweaty hands on his old army pants. "There's a leak," he said.

"A leak?" This was Ryan.

"In the organization," Ronny said. "Not just in the ranks. The big guys, at the top—they were getting busted. The guys who ran the big money and, you know, the stuff."

That probably meant drugs, I figured. If Dad was working for a bigger organization, then stolen cars were probably just a part of it. The big money was always in drugs.

"They were starting to panic at the top," Ronny said. "They didn't know who was ratting to the cops. There was a rumor for a while that it was you, Jace."

Jace hadn't said anything so far in this little excursion, but now he turned and looked at Ronny, and his eyes were like chips of ice. I'd never seen my brother's eyes like that. "I just did twenty months inside," he said. "I got a cavity search on my way in the door, and now I piss into a cup for a parole officer. And you think I'm a snitch?"

Ronny twitched again. "No, man, no," he said. "I don't think that. No one does. It was just panic, you know, trying to find someone to blame. And Dex was a cop—"

"Dex is not a cop," Jace said, his voice so cold that even Dex shut his mouth for once.

"Sure, sure," Ronny said. "Right, Jace, that's right. Anyway, it was just talk. There were all these arrests. And one night Mike got drunk and decided it was me who was the snitch. Me! I've been working with him for six years, and we've both made money, and suddenly he decides I'm the one talking to the cops! It was fucking outrageous."

"So he hit you with his car," I said.

"We were at the Barn, and it got heated, so we took it out back. Mike was drunk as hell. He had it in his head that it was me. He was convinced. Eventually he got in his car and revved it and aimed it right at me. I couldn't believe what the fuck was happening. I tried to run, but I wasn't fast enough." He looked down at his boot.

I looked out the window and saw that Dex had, after all, taken the turnoff onto Line Five, toward the quarry. It was a two-lane road to nowhere leading out of Westlake, bare of lights and blistered with potholes. The SUV gave a low growl as Dex accelerated.

Ronny noticed, too. "What are you doing? Where are we going? Come on, man!"

This wasn't part of the plan. Dex was improvising, like he'd done all his life. It went without saying that we shouldn't be doing this. And suddenly, I didn't fucking care.

When you come from the wrong side of the tracks, you get to stir the shit every once in a while.

I grabbed Ronny's collar to get his attention. "Names," I growled at him. "I want everyone's names—the guys at the top, the guys in the middle, everyone. I want to know everything you know."

"I can't do that," Ronny said. The SUV picked up speed and bounced hard over a pothole, nearly sending all of our skulls into the ceiling. In front, Ryan cursed, worried about his precious car. On the other side of Ronny, Jace swiveled to look back out the window, checking for cops. His eyes were worried but his jaw was set.

"Names," I said to Ronny again, "or Dex drives us all into the quarry."

"Yeehaw!" Dex shouted from the driver's seat. He steered with his pinky finger while he took a joint from his pocket and lit it, the sweet smoke filling the car. Ryan grabbed the wheel from him, cursing again.

"This is fucking nuts!" Ronny shouted. He was sweating like a fountain. "These are gangsters! Dangerous guys! You're messing with the wrong people!"

"Dex," I shouted, "did you hear that? These are dangerous guys."

"I'm fucking terrified," Dex said, and he drove the SUV over another pothole, jostling us all into the roof again. "Dangerous fucking guys!" he shouted. "Dangerous fucking guys!"

I barked a laugh; I couldn't help it. Dex was nuts. Maybe it was only funny if you didn't care about driving off the edge of a quarry in the last minutes of your life, but I laughed anyway.

The SUV went over another bump and something started rattling in the undercarriage. I thought Ryan would be pissed, but instead he turned around from the passenger seat and grabbed Ronny by the front of his shirt. "I left my kid everything," he said, his wild eyes staring right into Ronny's terrified ones. "Every penny. I don't give a shit about gangsters, and neither do my brothers. Dex is going to drive us all into the quarry. I'm telling you, *he'll do it*. Now *give us the fucking information*."

"Jace," Dex said. "You see any cops back there?"

"No cops," Jace said. "Go faster, Dex."

"Yessir," Dex said, giving a salute while squinting into the dark through the smoke from his joint. Then he floored it even harder. "Was that a sign for the quarry?" he shouted over the roar of the engine.

"It was," Jace shouted back. "Go faster. Let's go down quick."

"Okay! *Okay!*" Ronny was screaming so loud his voice broke. "Okay!" he screamed again in a rasp. "I'll talk! I'll talk! Just stop!"

We were actually approaching the quarry—that wasn't a lie. Dex was driving straight for it at top speed. My heart was racing and my breath was short, but the adrenaline high was so hard I didn't feel much else. In that moment, he could have driven us over like he promised, and I would probably have just floated into oblivion. My only regret would have been that I'd miss seeing Emily Parker naked in my bed ever again.

But Dex couldn't make anything easy. He hit the brakes and turned the wheel, and we spun hard, throwing gravel and dirt up from under the SUV's tires. The spin seemed to last and last, and then we were stopped, the SUV rocking on its frame. The broken-down chain link fence that circled the quarry was tangled over our rear end, and we were on an angle because one rear tire was actually over the edge of the quarry, its rim staring into the blackness below.

Ryan was still holding Ronny's shirt. Jace and I were braced against our doors. Dex turned around and looked at Ronny, squinting through the weed smoke again. His gaze was calm, dark, and empty, like a shark's.

"Spill," he said.

Ronny needed no more prompting; he started to talk. He talked and talked and talked. He named names. He told us everything there was to know, and Ronny Red knew a lot more than anyone gave him credit for.

Now we knew it, too.

When he was done we drove Ronny back into town and we dumped him in the Barn parking lot, shaking and trying not to puke. Dex wanted to leave him out by the quarry, but for once the rest of us outvoted him. Even a Riggs has to have some manners, after all.

"I take it back," Dex said when Ronny had gone and we all got out of Ryan's SUV in the Barn's empty lot. The SUV was filthy, the back end was scratched to shit, something was definitely rattling, and one of the tires was going flat. "The car isn't so bad. You still have a tiny dick, though."

"I hate every last fucking one of you," Ryan said.

For the Riggs brothers, that passed for a farewell.

We all went home.

TWENTY

Emily

THEY SAID a heat wave was starting, early in the year for Michigan. It was still ten days to the Fourth of July. It was going to be a long, hot summer.

Luke wasn't home at eight in the morning, even though I pounded on his back door. I remembered he used to go running in high school—he used to tell me it was the only thing that could get him out of bed before ten o'clock in the morning. Since he still had the awesome physique he'd had then, I guessed that was where he was and sat on his back porch to wait.

I was right. He showed up fifteen minutes later, wearing athletic shorts and a navy blue T-shirt that was nearly black with sweat. It was already almost eighty degrees, windless and still, and Luke's hair was soaked, sweat glistening on his arms and his collarbones.

He paused in surprise when he saw me. "Em," he said.

I looked at him for a long second. I couldn't help it. My head was full and my stomach hurt, but I would never get tired of looking at Luke Riggs. When I was ninety, I'd still like looking at him. It was time to accept that was just the way I was wired.

He stepped up onto the back porch, approaching where I sat on the old picnic table. He grabbed a towel from the spot on the porch, where he'd obviously left it, and scrubbed his face as I took him in. Muscled legs, lean hips, that stomach I'd admired and licked just days ago. Those sexy arms and capable hands, the tat I knew so well. Part of me was still amazed I'd actually slept with him—it seemed like a fantasy I'd cooked up in the middle of the night to wish it were true.

So I made myself say the words. "Today is the day."

He ran the towel over his neck. "Today is what day?"

"The day you get busted," I said. "The Westlake PD are going to raid Riggs Auto. They have warrants and everything." He went still, watching me with his dark eyes, so I dropped my gaze to my knees. "I overheard Mom talking on the phone last night. They're shutting you down, Luke. Your whole stolen car operation."

He heard the harshness in my voice on those last few words, because he said, "*My* stolen car operation?"

"That's what it is, isn't it?" I said, putting my hands on my knees and staring at them. "Mom says you're running it while your dad is in prison. You and your brothers. She says you're running at least five stolen cars a week through Riggs Auto. That it's part of a bigger organized crime circle." I traced the rings on my left hand with the fingers of my right. "One of your... employees got caught trying to fence a stolen watch. The watch was traced back to a car that was lifted last week. So they know the car has been through your operation. Your guy is arrested. It's a done deal."

He was quiet, so I gathered my courage and lifted my gaze to him. He was just standing there looking at me, the towel still in his hand. I couldn't read everything in his eyes—puzzlement, anger, maybe a flash of hurt. But that didn't make sense. What did he have to hurt about?

"Were you going to tell me?" I asked him, letting the words float out into the still, hot air. "Were you ever going to tell me what was going on?"

I'd suspected. Lauren had told me what Mom was working on, and I knew Luke's dad was not a good guy. But that was Mike. That wasn't Luke—at least in my mind. Luke was different.

I'd asked, and he'd told me next to nothing.

But this, an arrest, a big police bust... This made it real. It *was* Luke doing these things. Not just his father.

Luke's eyes narrowed. "Your mother has been investigating Riggs Auto for months. Were you ever going to tell me about that?"

"I'm telling you right now," I said.

"Yeah?" He slung the towel over his shoulder, then was still again. "Why, Emily? Why exactly are you telling me?"

That was a good question. I'd spent most of last night wide awake, pondering it. I should have just let the cops descend without warning, let Luke and the others go down like they were supposed to. What was happening was illegal—it was black and white. I should have just stood by and let the law do its work.

Instead, I was here.

"I don't know," I told him. "I guess I wanted to give you the chance to leave town."

His eyebrows rose at that. "Leave town?"

I shrugged. How was I supposed to know how criminals handled things? "I guess. You can leave town right now and avoid the whole thing." Of course he'd want to do that. Who would willingly walk into a police bust?

"Really," Luke said, but it wasn't a question. "You think I'd do that. Get in my car and just drive off."

I frowned at him. I didn't repeat that he'd done exactly that eight years ago. "You're going to jail if you don't."

"Yeah, you're probably right," he said.

I was starting to get angry. He was so fucking blah about the whole thing, like it didn't matter. I'd been up all night in agony, and to him it was a detail. "So that's it?" I said, my temper flaring in my voice. "You don't care about going to jail just like your dad? Were a few stolen cars worth it?"

"You think I'm willing to throw everything away for a bit of money?" Luke asked.

"I don't know," I snapped, "because you don't *tell* me anything. All we do is screw."

He took a step forward, and I could see that I'd pissed him off. "Then I'll tell you. Here's what happened. Dad called me up after eight years and said I had to take over Riggs Auto because he was going to jail. So I came back. It turns out Dad wasn't only a shitty father, he was a career criminal, and he assumed I'd be happy to take over. All the guys who work at Riggs are on board. There's already money being dropped in my lap that I didn't ask for. I've been dealing with the house, the business, my brothers, and you, and I've had to make some serious decisions. And I've had two weeks."

I stared at him, still angry. "Yeah, Luke. That's a lot to deal with. And you couldn't talk to me about any of it?"

"Honestly, Em?" He scowled at me. "You live with your mother. I was supposed to put you in that position?"

I knew what he meant. If I knew what was happening at Riggs Auto, it put me in the position of knowing something and not telling Mom about it. Or telling her and betraying Luke. Really, it put me in the position of having to choose between Mom and Luke.

I was in that position anyway. And I'd chosen Luke. By being here right now, giving him a warning, I was choosing him. And yet it still felt like an insult, even to me.

"Fine," I said to him. "You didn't choose any of this. It sucks. Now you can leave town and get away from all of it."

"You mean run," Luke said, and disdain dripped from his voice.

"Yes, I mean run!" I stood up, exasperated. "Or not. You know, I don't care. Since I'm probably an accessory by being here, I have to go."

I brushed past him, headed for the porch stairs. He didn't touch me, but I passed close enough to hear his low voice. "You're doing an awful lot for me when all we do is screw."

I paused and looked at him. I wanted to touch him so bad it was like an ache. Just put my palms on his chest, feel the heat of him, his heart beating, the rise and fall of his breath. Touching him was so familiar by now, it was almost like touching myself. Running my hands over his skin was like running them over my own. Touching Luke was a simple thing for me, body to body. We had entire conversations with just our hands and the feel of his breath on my skin. We fit. We always had.

But when I looked at him, I had no idea what he would do next. Whether or not he would get in his Charger and drive away again, keep driving and never look back. I honestly didn't know.

Did I?

I had to keep some distance here. I had to stay hard. Because this man could break me, and one way or the other, I didn't know if I'd ever see him again. And I couldn't let that crack me open. I had to stay strong, together. I had to stay me.

"Good luck, Luke," I said, and walked away through the back route to my car. For the last time.

TWENTY-ONE

Luke

AFTER THAT, things went just about as expected. That is, they went to shit.

It was never going to be a good day.

By noon I was sitting in a little room, windowless and stuffy, with the air conditioning wheezing through the vents, bringing barely a puff of cool air. I was seated in a plastic chair in front of a small wooden table, and there was a plastic cup filled with water sitting on the table, the water sweating down the sides of the glass. It was a hot fucker of a day, a mean kind of hot, with smog-colored clouds that tinged the sky and air that smelled like an armpit. What the day needed was a bitch of a storm to blow through and blow everything away.

The door of the room opened and a cop came through, a middle-aged guy in uniform. "Riggs," he said.

I looked at him. "Get me Nora Parker," I said.

He shook his head. "That's not going to happen."

"Am I under arrest?"

"No," he said. "But we really, really suggest you answer our questions."

"Then I really, really suggest you get me Nora Parker. Or I'm not answering a damn thing."

He looked mad, but there was nothing he could do about it. We both knew it. He turned around and left again.

I waited, and the water sweated down the sides of the plastic cup.

At long last, she came. Nora Parker wasn't wearing a uniform; she'd been promoted out of the uniform ranks, though I had no idea what the police ranks even were. She wore dress pants and a light blue blouse, and her hair was tied back in a braid. She was tall and elegant like Lauren, but her eyes were exactly Emily's, the color and shape of them. It made me ache to look into those eyes, so I did it again and again.

All we do is screw.

Nora pulled out the chair across from me and sat down. She didn't look very pleased to be talking to me, but she was almost painfully alert, taking in every detail of me. She was keyed up, because today was a big day. I wondered what she saw when she looked at me, just like I wondered what Emily saw when she looked at me. Deep down, I didn't think I wanted to know.

She put a pad of paper and a pen on the table in front of her. "Hello, Luke," she said. Her voice was different from Emily's, calm and melodious. But still a Parker woman voice, with that backbone of steel.

"Officer Parker," I said.

"It's sergeant, actually," she said.

I didn't say anything to that. We looked at each other across the table.

"You thirsty?" she asked me, motioning to the cup of water. "It's hot."

"Your air conditioning doesn't work so good," I said.

"Yeah, we really need it fixed."

I almost smiled at that. Almost. Need the air conditioning fixed, my ass. It was probably a psychological tactic. They were trying to sweat me, literally.

She and I stared at each other for another minute. Me and Emily's mother.

"Do I need a lawyer?" I asked her, though I already knew the answer.

"Do you want one?" she countered. "I suppose you can call one, though you're just here for questioning. You're not under arrest."

No, I wasn't. Because they had nothing to arrest me for. The cops had come to Riggs Auto, just like Emily had said they would. They'd come to the front door with a warrant, and they'd marched right in, a whole team of them. It was impressive work.

But they hadn't found anything. There were no stolen cars in the garage, and none parked out back either. When they'd handed me the warrant to search my house, I knew they'd find nothing there either. I'd moved the money from the second safe, stashed it. Even if the cops had the combination, they'd find nothing.

So I wasn't under arrest. But Tim Cleaver was. That was the guy who'd tried to sell a stolen watch at a jeweller's. It was a dumb idea. I always knew it was the stolen goods that would bring the whole thing down.

They couldn't arrest me, because they had no charges. But they could sit me in this room and sweat me. For as long as they wanted, really. Actually, right now that was fine with me. Because I didn't want to get out of here and go home, or go back to Riggs Auto. I didn't have anywhere that I wanted to go.

All we do is screw.

I looked at the pen and paper in front of Nora Parker. "Are

we being recorded?" I asked. There were no windows in this room, so I already knew there was no one-way glass.

She smiled a little at that. "No," she said. "Westlake is a small police department. We don't have a budget for secret recordings. When we need to talk to someone, we just sit face to face and ask them. And if we need to record the conversation, we have a recorder we bring in the room with us."

She was telling the truth, I could tell. There were obviously no cameras in this little room. All that stuff from *Law and Order* didn't really happen in Westlake.

Which made this a private conversation. So I said, "I've been seeing Emily for the past two weeks."

For a second her face went slack with shock. Then she reassembled her expression, admirably I thought. "Seeing," she said, picking a word out of what I'd said.

There was no reason to be coy. "Sleeping with," I said.

Her expression got a little hard at that, but she was watching me closely, and she believed me. "I knew she was seeing someone," she admitted, the mother in her coming out for just a brief second. "So. You."

"Me," I said. I broke my gaze away from her and stared at the wall, at nothing, making the thoughts come together. I made myself say the words, because they were important. "I love her," I told Nora. "I'm in love with her. However you want to put it. I shouldn't be, but I am." I rearranged the words, tried to make her understand. "I want to be the kind of guy who deserves her."

When I made myself look back at her, she'd put her neutral cop's expression on again. But I could see past it, just a crack. Those words meant something to her. Just a little bit, but something.

"I know," I said to her, "I'm Mike Riggs' son. I'm not that guy. And maybe she'll never talk to me again. But I still decided I want to be that guy, the guy who deserves her even if he doesn't get a shot. That's the guy I want to be. That's all I want to be."

She frowned at me. "Luke?"

"You're doing really good," I told her. "You and your team, whoever you're working with. You're on the right track. Your guy on the inside is leaking good information, and you've got them scared."

Nora blinked. "What?"

"The arrests freaked them out," I said. "It made them change tactics, that's all. They shut down the warehouse on Meadowvale Avenue. They cleared it out, because they figured it was a dirty site, that you guys would be knocking on the door any day."

"We're aware of the warehouse," she said in a guarded voice.

I shook my head. "You can raid it all you want, but you won't find anything. They've moved to the old sugar refinery off Route Two. You know the one?"

She seemed a little stunned, but she nodded once.

"The loading dock in the back," I said. "That's where we deliver the cars when we're done with them. Big Jim does most of it, but you probably already know that." They'd taken away Big Jim when they'd taken me, and he was probably sitting in a cell, waiting for his turn in this hot little room. "The guy who delivers the car to us is named Dave Matthews, like the band. He works as the car wash place on Roosevelt Avenue, the one with all the soap suds on the sign. Car delivery is what he does as a side gig. He's probably there now."

Nora pulled the pad of paper to her and made a note, then another. She wrote for a minute, then looked up at me again. "Luke, where's the money?"

"We got a drop two days ago," I said. "The guy who drops the money is named Gus White. He's a big bald guy. He works for another guy named Dennis Mitchell." I watched her expression flinch as I said the name, because she knew it. He was one of the bigger fish in the organization. "Gus knows the security code at Riggs and he drops the money in the safe out back. The last drop was one hundred and fifty thousand, exactly."

"And where is that hundred and fifty thousand now?"

"I tracked down Gus White and gave it back to him. I told him to give it back to his boss." I shrugged. "What he actually did with it, I couldn't say."

She stared at me in shock. "You had a face-to-face meeting with Gus White?"

"I have resources." It was Dex who had tracked down Gus and set up the meeting, using his contacts. But I was leaving my brothers out of this.

Gus had been pretty chill, actually, about the fact that I was telling him not to have cars sent through Riggs Auto anymore. That we were out of business.

He could have been pissed off about it. He could have killed me, even. But people are usually chill when you're handing them money and not the other way around.

"Okay," Nora said, "I admit that's impressive. The guys who run the old warehouse—the sugar refinery, I mean. Do you have names?"

"I have names."

"Jesus, it's like Christmas in June," she said. "We've questioned Ron Ruvinsky more than once. The man who calls himself Ronny Red. He's never told us anything."

I shrugged. The cops didn't have the Riggs brothers' interrogation tactics.

"In any case," Nora went on, "Ronny Red has left town. No one knows where he went. We also interviewed your father before he was arrested for trying to kill Ronny. We had him sitting in that same chair you're in four times. He never had a single thing to tell us."

I ran a hand through my hair. "Yeah, well, I'm not him."

"I'm starting to see that."

"No, you don't," I said. "Maybe you'll never see it. It doesn't matter, really. Maybe you'll never have to see me again. Or maybe Emily will give me a shot and you'll be stuck with me. That isn't up to either of us."

A frown appeared between her eyebrows. "Luke, if you love her like you say..." She trailed off.

"Then what?" I asked.

Nora shook her head. "Good God, a Riggs boy," she said softly to herself. She pinched the bridge of her nose with her fingers and closed her eyes. "Of all the men in the world for my daughter to fall in love with."

My heart did a slow turn in my chest, but I was quiet. I waited. If Emily was actually in love with me, I could wait a long time.

Besides, even though it was insulting, I got it. If I had a daughter, I'd be pissed if she ended up with a guy like me.

Well, that was just too bad.

Nora sighed and opened her eyes. "If you love her like you say, then this was the right thing to do." She picked up her notebook and pen and stood, heading for the door.

"That's it?" I forced the words out. "I'm free to go?"

She turned back. "I see no evidence of criminal activity on your part," she said—a little reluctantly, I thought. "You seem like a good guy who is trying to do the right thing. I try not to make a habit of locking guys like that up."

I narrowed my eyes at her. "That sounds like bullshit."

"Does it?" she said coolly. "It is, a little. I'm going to check every part of this out. I'm going to check *you* out. And my PD knows who you are, where you are. We know what you're doing. If you try to leave town, there will be an APB before you can hit Road Six."

"That's more like it," I said. I pushed my chair back and stood up. "I'm getting out of this fucking hot room and going home."

Nora paused and caught my gaze with hers. "Tell her," she said quietly. "Emily probably doesn't know how you feel. She puts on a tough exterior, but on the inside she's vulnerable." Then she turned, and walked out the door.

TWENTY-TWO

Emily

I DIDN'T CALL HIM.

I wasn't going to call him.

I left Luke that morning and went to the salon, driving the car he'd fixed for a measly hundred bucks. Maybe he'd been generous because he didn't need any more money. Maybe he already had plenty from moving stolen cars through the body shop business. Maybe he had wads of money stashed away, and more coming in. Maybe his brothers did, too. I didn't know, did I? I didn't really know Luke at all.

But I didn't think that was true. I didn't *think* Luke had a bunch of illegal money stashed away. I didn't *think* he'd come home and taken over for his no-good father. I didn't think he'd been fencing stolen cars by day while he was sleeping with me at night. *We just don't know what to fucking do,* he'd said that night when the cops were parked at the end of his driveway. The only time he'd talked to me about it even a little. He'd sounded torn. Like he could go in one direction, or he could go in another.

The question was, which direction had he taken?

I worked all day at the salon on autopilot, barely registering anything around me. When I went home, Mom wasn't home. With the big bust at Riggs Auto, she was probably working late. And I hadn't heard from Lauren, either; she was busy with her own life. So was Dad.

I rummaged the fridge for leftovers and watched TV alone. In my mind's eye, I pictured where Luke was right now. Option one: in jail. Option two: far away somewhere, driving his Charger, the trunk loaded with cash. It was a silly Hollywood image, but I had it anyway.

I tried to picture a third option, but every time I came up with something awful. Luke shot by cops; Luke hurt somehow; Luke dead. My silent phone was torture. If Luke was hurt or dead, no one would call me, because no one knew we were together. No one would know I cared.

We had gone wrong somewhere. Was it my fault? His? From the minute he picked me up by the side of the road I'd been in a spin, and not just because my life was a temporary mess. If I'd come home that day and told everyone that Luke was my boyfriend, if I'd let everyone in town know, like I now knew I wanted to do—would things have turned out differently? Or would everything have happened exactly the same?

I picked up my phone a thousand times. *Where are you?* I typed it over and over, but I never hit send. Because what if I didn't like the answer? What if he didn't answer at all?

I lay on the sofa as the hour got later and later. I turned off the TV, tired of pretending to watch it when there was no one to fool. I curled on my side and lay there, sick to my stomach, tears leaking onto the sofa cushion beneath my cheek.

I couldn't do this. This was why I'd pushed all thoughts of

Luke into that closed-door room for eight years—because right now everything hurt. I'd tried so hard to find a guy who wasn't like Luke. A guy who was normal, who had a job and a regular upbringing, who wanted normal things, who wasn't a rebel and a wanderer and probably a criminal. Because I'd always known that loving Luke would be hard, that it would come with hard decisions, and that those decisions would hurt.

I loved him anyway.

But I wouldn't call him. Because he could ruin me.

I drifted toward sleep, and the last thought I had before I went out was that I didn't think that Luke had run.

He could have, but I didn't think he had. I'd bet my life on it.

And then I was gone.

I WOKE up to the sound of the coffee maker percolating. I rolled over on the sofa and saw that it was still dark out.

I stood and walked to the kitchen, where the light was on. Mom was there, fully dressed for work, pouring herself a cup of coffee. The clock on the stove said it was five a.m.

Mom turned and looked at me. She took in what a wreck I must have looked like. "Sweetie," she said.

And I broke. I finally broke. "What happened?" I said, my voice cracking. "Please tell me."

Mom sipped her coffee, watching me over the brim. In that moment she was a mom, and she was also a very good cop at the same time. She'd always been able to pull that off, being a mom and a cop at once. "You're worried about Luke," she said.

I stared at her.

She nodded, sipped her coffee again. "We have a lot to talk about," she said. "Starting with the topic of Luke Riggs."

"Is he okay?" I asked.

"The last I saw, he was fine," Mom said.

I forced the words out. "And when was that?"

"Yesterday, in the interrogation room at the station." She watched my face. "Someday, my girl, I'm going to find out exactly what you knew and when you knew it."

This was the situation Luke had tried to avoid: me having to choose between Mom and him. I rubbed my fingers over my cheeks, feeling the dried-up tear tracks. "I knew that he came home and found out what his father was into," I said. "He wouldn't tell me anything else. That's the truth."

Mom watched me carefully, then sipped her coffee again. "Trying not to put you in the middle," she said. "He really is a smart boy. I would never have guessed that Mike Riggs could have a son who was that smart. Good-looking, too."

Was Mom complimenting him? That couldn't be right. "Is he in jail?" I asked, because I couldn't take not knowing anymore.

"No," Mom said. She frowned into her coffee cup, not noticing how I sagged with relief. "In fact, he was rather wonderful."

"Wonderful?" I couldn't have heard right.

"Yes, I know," Mom said. "The Riggs boys are many things, but wonderful isn't one of them. But I'm a big enough person to admit that he sat in that interrogation room and handed me a huge chunk of my investigation. If he's telling the truth about all of it, I'll likely get promoted. At the very least, he made my job much, much easier."

It sunk in, what she was saying. Luke hadn't left, and he hadn't been arrested. He'd told Mom everything he knew.

It could have gotten him arrested. If he ratted on the wrong people, it could have gotten him killed. It still could. And he'd done it anyway.

And he'd told Mom about him and me. He had to have said something, because she knew.

"What did he say about me?" I asked.

"You'll have to ask him that," Mom said. "But you know, I'm not a cop for nothing. From what he said, and from how you look right now, I think you two have known each other for longer than two weeks. Am I right?"

Oh, God. It was going to come out, all of it. Including the beginning of the story, when we were eighteen.

And that didn't scare me anymore. Instead, I felt a quiet rush of something behind my breastbone. Excitement, maybe. And a little bit of hope.

"I'll tell you everything," I said to her. "I'll tell you the whole story." *Except for the explicit sex parts.* "But I'll do it later. Right now I'm going to go clean up."

"Yes, and I have to go to work," Mom said. "I got in late and I'm starting early. Time to put the bad guys away." She smiled. Her marriage might break up and life might happen to her daughters, but Mom's work had always made her happy. She was born to be a cop. She was a fucking hero.

"I love you, Mom," I said, my voice cracking.

"I love you too, honey." She touched my cheek. "Try not to wreck him. I meant what I said. He really is good-looking."

"Mom."

"I'm a cop. I have powers of observation. And if you two work it out, ask him to dinner."

TWENTY-THREE

Emily

IT WAS a busy day at The Big Do. All six chairs were occupied with regulars, plus two more customers at the manicure station. Mrs. Lipnicki was sitting on the side sofa with a coffee next to her, reading a magazine and waiting for the next chair to be free. The rep from the salon products line was here, going over the inventory we might stock for the next three months. Since it was such an important decision, Lauren had come into the shop for the meeting, and the three of us were standing by the front reception, me answering the phone and greeting clients, listening in to Lauren and the rep talking when I could.

My stomach rumbled. I'd been too upset and tired this morning to eat breakfast, and my stomach was still in knots at lunch. Now it was almost dinnertime, and I was hungry. I felt stretched thin, able to think about the basics and not much else. I needed to talk to Luke, but work didn't slow down for things like that. Work didn't stop because I didn't know where I stood with the guy I was in love with.

Lauren kept shooting me concerned looks, but she looked stretched thin herself. She and Vic were going to sell their house in the divorce, and she was busy cleaning it out, preparing it for sale, and dealing with the real estate agent, plus finding somewhere else to live. I had a feeling she'd be in her own single bed in her room next to mine at Mom's house before too long. At least we'd be humiliated together.

I had just hung up the phone yet again and was trying to follow the discussion of dry shampoos when the bell over the door rang.

The hair on the back of my neck prickled, just like it had that day at the gas station. A couple of the conversations in the shop died in surprise. The product rep stopped talking. I turned around.

Luke was standing there.

He was wearing a black button-down shirt, jeans, and boots. His dark hair was clean and tousled and his beard was trimmed. He looked big and very, very male in the middle of the salon, and his gaze was fixed on me. More of the conversations around me went quiet.

I felt the breath rush out of me. I moved around the reception desk without thinking, putting nothing between me and him.

"Emily?" Lauren said.

I ignored her. I was looking at Luke, and nothing could make me look away.

"Are you all right?" I asked him.

His gaze burned over me, down and up again. My sundress and my light cardigan nearly vanished in smoke. I squirmed my toes in my sandals.

"I'm still in town," Luke said in his low drawl.

"I see that," I managed.

"You think I'd fucking leave you?" Luke said.

From behind me in the salon, one of the women said, "Oh, sweet baby Jesus."

The place had gone quiet; everyone was looking, listening. In the window of the shop door, people walked by on the street. We were in the middle of downtown Westlake. Luke and me. In public. In full view.

"I'm sorry," I said. "I knew you wouldn't run. I just didn't know..." I glanced past his shoulder at the street outside, where a cop cruiser glided by, slowly. "Who is that?" I asked.

Luke didn't even have to turn and look. "My escort," he said, "courtesy of Sergeant Parker. So far today they've followed me to the bank and watched while I got gas. Seems they don't want me to leave town."

"You have cops following you around?"

"I'm just that kind of guy," Luke said. When I bit my lip and stared at him, he said, "You okay with that?"

He was asking if that was what I wanted. If *he* was what I wanted. Like I'd say he wasn't good enough and kick him out the door. I wanted to kiss him, and I wanted to shake him. For a minute I was robbed of speech.

Behind me in the salon, one of the women said, "Say you're okay with it, honey."

"I'm okay with it," I said to Luke.

"Good," Luke said. He stepped forward and boxed me in against the reception desk, his arms on either side of me. "I figure if the cops want to know my business, they might as well learn it. My business is you."

"What the hell," Lauren said from behind my shoulder. "I *knew* it."

"Damn, woman," one of the salon customers added. "Jump on that. I would."

My cheeks were hot, but I wasn't embarrassed. Not even a

little. This felt right. After so much time sneaking around and hiding, pretending we weren't what we were, I felt something rise and flutter in my chest. Happiness. Like I was finally showing the world who I really was.

I put my hand on Luke's jaw, feeling the rough smoothness of his beard. I ran it down the side of his neck, tucked my fingertips inside the fold of his collar. He was big and warm and vital and mine. "I told you we weren't over," I said to him, trying to keep my voice from breaking. "I meant it."

"We'll never be over," Luke said. And he leaned in and kissed me.

I kissed him back, one hand on his neck, curling my other hand into his hair. He lifted his hands from the reception desk and put them on the small of my back, bringing my body to his as I opened my mouth. The women in the salon hooted and yelled.

"Jesus," Lauren said.

The door bell rang behind us as another customer walked in. "Oh my," she said.

We broke off before we gave everyone too much of a show, but Luke didn't take his hands from my back. "You hungry?" he asked me.

"I'm starving," I said, because he knew I was. "Let's go to dinner."

"Where?"

"Aria's." It was a nice restaurant three blocks from here, a date place, and I'd always wanted to go.

"Okay," Luke said. He dropped his hands from my back and took my hand in his instead. He looked past my shoulder at my sister. "Emily's leaving now," he said. "She won't be back tonight."

I turned to see my sister with her jaw dropped. She made an effort to close her mouth. Beside her, the product rep had her arms crossed over her chest and a grin on her face. "Okay," Lauren said faintly.

"Oh, and Lauren," I said, "I should tell you. I'm dating Luke Riggs."

"Okay," Lauren said again, and then she recovered enough to narrow her eyes at me. "I'm calling you later."

"Not later," I corrected her. "Tomorrow."

"Damn right!" one of the women shouted, and someone else applauded. And we left the salon to walk to Aria's.

After eight years, I was on a date with Luke Riggs.

And it was the only place I wanted to be.

TWENTY-FOUR

Luke

Two months later

I RAN my hand down Emily's bare back, tracing my fingers down her spine. Her skin was damp with late-summer-sex sweat, but she still shivered under my touch.

"That feels nice," she said into the pillow, her relaxed post-orgasm voice. "Do you think anyone heard us?"

"Probably," I said, running my fingers over her again. "You're loud, babe."

"I can't help it," she said. "You know I like it when you bend me over like that."

I brushed her hair away from her neck and leaned in and kissed her warm skin. "I like it when you suck my cock," I said in her ear, "but I don't make noise like that."

She squirmed. "You make more noise than you think you do. I hope Jace has noise cancelling headphones."

I smiled against her skin. Jace had moved out of the halfway house and was now living in the guest house. We'd made it up nice for him, with all new furniture. The guest house was private and quiet, but I had the bedroom window partly open to catch the breeze, and it was possible the sound had carried.

The main house was just for us—because Emily lived here now. It hadn't taken us long to decide that she should move out of her mother's place and in with me. It had seemed like the natural next move, and it was working out perfectly. We'd wasted enough time already.

I put a hand on Emily's hip and rolled her onto her back. She was always extra pliant after I made her come, and she let me do it. I propped my head on my hand and looked down at her. It was Sunday afternoon, the best time—in my opinion—for lazy, hot, drawn-out sex with my girlfriend. When I could see every inch of her.

"You have to work tomorrow?" I asked.

She groaned softly. "Yes. We're getting the new coloring chemicals in. The shipment arrives at eight, and I have to be there."

Emily wasn't just running her sister's salon anymore; she was now part owner. Lauren's divorce was almost final, but she said she was burned out on the business and still wanted time off. Emily, on the other hand, was a natural at running the shop, and loved doing it. My girl liked to be her own boss.

So the two sisters had worked out a deal: Emily ran the place, while Lauren was more of a silent partner, helping with the big decisions only. Emily took a bigger share of the profits, but Lauren still got a cut. After six months, if Lauren still didn't want to come back, Emily would own the place outright.

It was an arrangement that worked for both of them.

"What are you going to do?" Emily asked me.

I traced a fingertip over her bare collarbone. "Jace and I will go into Riggs Auto. Try to get it ready to open next week."

After the busts, I'd closed Riggs Auto indefinitely. Everyone who worked there was either arrested or fired. No more stolen cars came through there, and eventually the heat from the cops died down. Nora Parker had her arrests, she had her credit, and she had her promotion.

And yeah, I went to dinner at Detective Parker's house. Often. We got along fine, in fact. Because she was Emily's mother, and Emily mattered to me.

I'd done side work over the last two months to make money, taking in repairs and doing them myself in the closed down body shop. But Jace was back now, and he needed a job. And we had customers—real ones—who wanted to come back. And hell, who knew, maybe we could even get new customers if we opened up again and did it right.

So we were working on it, Jace and me. Clearing out the confusing piles of paper and putting a computer in the body shop's office. Figuring out credit cards and sales taxes and all the other shit Dad had always done under the table. We'd looked at new equipment and cleaning the shop out, getting rid of the old junkers that didn't run and made the shop look shitty. We were even considering getting a new sign.

We had the money, after all. It was sitting in the safe deposit box in Detroit in envelopes with our names on it. Ryan had even given us his envelope to use, though Dex's share was gone. We figured the best use for Dad's dirty money was to fix up his dirty shop, completely against his instructions.

We Riggs brothers were legit, but not *that* legit.

Emily rolled off the bed and walked to the bathroom. I watched her go. It took her a little while to clean up in there, because we'd graduated to going bare—something I'd never done with any woman before. It was different, and it was fucking awesome. There was no feeling like coming bare inside your woman, even though we weren't trying to have kids. Not now, and maybe not ever. We were in no rush.

When she came out again, she picked up my discarded T-shirt from the floor and put it on. She sat on the bed and scrubbed a hand through her sex-tousled hair. "Do you think he's lonely back there?" she said.

"Who?"

"Jace." She ran a finger over the tattoo on my arm. "He's so quiet. He has no friends, no girl. He works and reads books by himself. He seems lonely."

"Getting out of prison is hard, babe," I said. "A lot of guys can't readjust."

She nodded, still tracing my tattoo. There was a worried frown between her eyes. "Maybe he should get some help."

"He is," I said. "They're sending him to some kind of counselor. He goes the day after tomorrow."

"Maybe that will be good," she allowed.

I tugged on her bent knee and pulled her across the covers toward me. "You worried about my brothers?" I asked.

She rolled her eyes and lay back against the pillows. "Only Jace," she said. "Ryan and Dex are hopeless."

I laughed. Ryan was still in Detroit with Dylan, and I had no idea where Dex was. Since it was Sunday afternoon, he was probably sleeping off last night's party. "Good," I said. "Jace is nice, but there's only one Riggs who's your business."

She looked up at me with those beautiful gray eyes, and she smiled. She hooked an arm around my neck. "You're my business," she said.

"Yeah," I told her. "I am."

Then I kissed her.

And we got down to business.

A NOTE FROM JULIE

Thank you for reading Drive Me Wild! I hope you enjoyed it!

Coming next in 2018:

Take Me Down (Jace's story)

Work Me Up (Ryan's story)

Make Me Beg (Dex's story)

You can find all of the updated information about my books, and you can sign up for my newsletter, at www.juliekriss.com.

Turn the page to find a list of my other books!

ALSO BY JULIE KRISS

The Bad Billionaire Series

Bad Billionaire

Dirty Sweet Wild

Rich Dirty Dangerous

Back in Black

Standalone

Spite Club

The Eden Hills Duet

Bad Boyfriend

Bad Wedding

DRIVE
ME WILD

Emily was a cop's daughter, and I was the boy from the wrong side of the tracks. At eighteen, our affair was wild and completely secret. Until she left town for college and a better life, and I hit the road to nowhere.

Eight years later, we're both back in town. My father is in prison; Emily is selflessly helping her sister. We should be further apart than we've ever been. But I've never been able to resist temptation, especially when that temptation is Emily.

I SHOULDN'T GO NEAR HER. BUT I DO.

SHE SHOULDN'T SAY YES. BUT SHE DOES.

Our chemistry is hotter than ever, but she's hiding something from me. Just like I'm hiding something from her. It's hard to tell whose secrets are more dangerous, until it all goes to hell.

I CAN SAVE HER - AND SHE CAN SAVE ME.
BUT WE'LL HAVE TO BREAK THE RULES.

WE'RE FROM DIFFERENT WORLDS.
WE DON'T BELONG TOGETHER.

But in the end, Emily and I are going to have to get dirty.

ISBN 9780995967595

90000

9 780995 967595